Tempus Militibus
By
Anna Daly McCabe

Tempus Militibus

A Tempus Militibus Novel, Volume 1

A D McCabe

Published by Mizen Publishing, 2024.

This is a work of fiction. Similarities to real people, places, or events are entirely coincidental.

TEMPUS MILITIBUS

First edition. May 31, 2024.

Copyright © 2024 A D McCabe.

ISBN: 979-8224642625

Written by A D McCabe.

For All Who Dream

A Tempus Militibus Novel
Book 1

Chapter 1

The panigale screamed as the throttle was rolled back a little further and the rider lifted it effortlessly onto the rear wheel. The power of the engine seared through the body of its master as they raced toward the McClure tunnel in Santa Monica.

Glancing momentarily in the side mirror, the rider could see that his follower was still chasing him, he grinned. It was proving almost impossible to rid himself of his companion, however he was enjoying the chase. He loved to challenge this bike at speed, and the bike never failed to respond to his command.

As he roared into the tunnel, the rider knew that he would have to rid himself of this haemorrhoid once and for all. He did have a meeting and he couldn't play all night, *even if he wanted to, and he did want to!*

Looking in the mirror once more, he saw that the other rider was getting close. *Good!*

He knew what he had to do. He took his hands off the bars and stood up and without hesitation he jumped from the moving bike. He twisted his body in a three-hundred-and-sixty-degree movement, as if in slow motion, his arms were outstretched as though he were flying in the face of the oncoming biker.

The motorbike slammed to the surface of the tunnel, emitting a bright crimson trail of sparks, that lit-up the tunnel bore.

Standing upright with his legs apart, the rider unsheathed his broad sword from under his long leather coat and rotating about, he stood poised ready to connect with the onrushing rider. *Come on!* He thought to himself. *What are you slowing for?*

The other rider was unable to react quickly enough, as the flat blade connected with his chest, and knocked him clean from the bike onto the tunnel surface. The rider slid on his back along the road surface for what seemed like an eternity.

In an instant the panigale rider was beside the stricken motorcyclist, he waved his sword in the air and the swishing sound reverberated in the tunnel. The scrambler tried to get up, but the sword was now inches from his jugular.

"Please..." He begged in a pleading voice. "I meant..." But from behind his helmet, the panigale rider just grinned. *That's right, beg!* He loved it. *Plead for your worthless life!*

"Requiem in inferno." The swordsman yelled as he brought the blade down with force on the fallen racer's neck, the sword sliced through bone and tissue, and the severed head of the rider rolled along the concrete surface for several paces. The assailant stood up and looked around. He had to react fast. The tunnel was empty. Quickly he pushed the bike over to the side of the road and picked up the torso of the fallen rider, he placed it beside the bike and then with two strides he was standing beside the head. With a tap of his right foot, he kicked the head, and it rolled over to the body.

For a few moments, he looked at the headless body and then he saw the bright light as it engulfed the head and the body until all that remained was a pile of soot. *Job done!*

He strode over to his own bike and picked it up by the handlebars and looked at the damage. It was extensive, this was worse than previous times. It would require considerable work to repair. But it did feel good at the time, it always did.

He threw his long leg over the bike, and it started first turn. The panigale roared into life and the rear wheel slid from side to side as he drove at speed out of the tunnel. He was back in control of the machine, and he loved it.

The ride to the body shop took only minutes as he maneuvered up to the door and glanced up at the camera. He raised his right hand and waited for the roller door to rise. He rolled the bike inside and switched off the engine and got off his damaged motorcycle.

Slowly he removed his helmet and shook his head, his long blond hair cascaded down the back of his long black leather coat like a silken mane. He was tall, six foot seven and he wore tight leather trousers, with leather boots buckled over his muscular calf. He wore no shirt under the trench coat, as was his preference when he went out on the panigale.

He didn't turn around immediately when the door opened, and someone came in. He smiled slowly as his companion came over to look at the machine.

"Praetorian," His deep voice called out as he turned around and looked at his friend. "What can you do with it?" He threw the helmet at his colleague, who caught it in one hand, his reflexes unquestionable.

"What happened?" He asked as he looked, with a pained expression at the custom built panigale and shook his head in utter disgust.

"I was chased by a fool." He said as he removed his sword and walked over to the bench and picked up a rag and began to wipe the black gooey substance from the blade. He grimaced, this was always a disgusting chore but one that had to be done.

"Was it necessary to destroy the bike?" His companion asked. "Such a beautiful machine, a work of art, have you any comprehension what you are doing to it?" The blond man turned and looked and him and nodded casually. "Lanny, that's the third time in two weeks that you've damaged this bike." Lanny stood up straight and flashed him a wicked smile.

"Praetorian, it's your job to fix it, besides you do a great job." Lanny grinned and held out the rag to him. "Now, when can I expect it?" He chortled as he looked at his friend, who was still shaking his head in despair at the damage done to the bike.

"I'll have it for you on Saturday," Lanny nodded and walked over to the door and opened it, then his friend turned to him and said casually. "But I should punish you and not fix it at all."

"The General and the Berserker are expecting us. Can you give me a lift?" He grinned as he faced his friend, "As I am now without transport." They left the garage together.

"I should make you walk, for destroying that beauty." The Praetorian said and laughed.

Chapter 2

Lanny strode in and confidently walked over to the fireplace. There was a fire, blazing in the grate. It was a little chilly outside, and he needed the warmth that the fire afforded him.

"You're late, what happened?" Luca asked as he raised the crystal glass to his mouth.

"Lanny, had an accident." The other man replied as he sat down on the sofa and leaned back. "Again!" Luca glanced at the tall man standing in front of the fire with his back to the room.

"What happened, Lanny?" Luca quizzed as he took another sip of whiskey.

"We have a small problem in the Downtown area." Lanny said and then turned to face the dark-haired man who was sitting upright on the antique armchair. "A small band of dregs, it looks like they just arrived in town. They recognised me as Militibus at once." He looked at the three men sitting in the room. "One of them decided to follow me so I led him to the tunnel and finished him off." He allowed himself to grin, he always enjoyed the chase, and the kill even more.

"Were you spotted?" Luca asked, his expression was bland. "In the tunnel?"

"I don't believe so, I didn't see any cameras, but would the camera have caught the action anyway?" Lanny replied with a grin. "Besides there was no traffic in the tunnel at the time."

"They don't usually travel in small packs." The man who was sitting in the other armchair, spoke. "Perhaps they were a scouting party." Lanny looked at him, he could be right. But he doubted it.

"Bjorn, when did you encounter the sucker?" Luca asked, unhurriedly as he raised the glass again.

"Two months ago." Bjorn said in a deep voice. "She was alone, there wasn't a pack."

"How can you be sure Berserker?" Lanny asked bellowing at Bjorn, he hated assumptions.

"When a female sucker is alone, it usually means she has been banished from the lair." Bjorn retorted as he glared at the Jarl.

"Not necessarily." Lanny said, almost sulkily, he didn't like being challenged or proven wrong in anything.

"I wonder why they are suddenly descending on the metropolis now." The question was directed at no one in particular.

"What are you saying, Praetorian?" Lanny asked. He was clearly irritated now and felt that it was a personal dig at him by the Berserker and the Praetorian, and he wasn't amused.

"Well, the last time we saw a pack of suckers enter the city was three maybe four years ago." Peo said as he crossed one leg over the other. "Something is up, and they are starting to descend on the city again. Question is, why?" They all agreed. This could mean a new case for them to investigate.

"We need to be vigilant, the last thing we need is to draw attention to ourselves amongst the police Downtown. The less we encounter Detective Sometti the better" Luca said and tapped his fingers on the cold leather of the armchair. "I'll check with Demis, find out if an event has happened." They nodded and then Bjorn asked.

"Why did you call this meeting, Luca?" He grinned. "So late at night too." The other three laughed. "It can't be about the wellbeing of the city."

"Well," Luca smiled impishly at his comrades. "I have had a new consignment of exceptional whiskey delivered this afternoon." Luca stood up. "So, let's drink some fine malt." He walked over to the cabinet and poured four glasses of the refined, rare Midleton whiskey for each of them. "Iubentium." He raised his glass and the four of them toasted. It was going to be a good night after all, Lanny thought as he raised his glass.

"Iubentium." He took a sip, one thing Luca had, that they all enjoyed without exception, was his love of rare and outstanding taste in spirits, tonight was no different.

Chapter 3

There was a hushed silence in the lobby as one of the benefactors, John Josess, a prominent businessman, turned on the microphone. He looked around at the many faces whom he recognised and some of whom he had done business with before. He was a greedy man, and he was thrilled to see the great turnout, these occasions were always profitable, for him at least.

"Thank you, ladies, and gentlemen," he said with a broad grin on his face. He really enjoyed these events. "Thank you all for coming here today. As you know, the hotel has been idle and neglected for many years, while on our streets, men, women and young people," he glanced around, looking concerned at those congregated in the opulent lobby. "Have been living down on skid row. Never knowing where they will be in the morning, or if they would be alive." He paused for effect. No one gathered, believed in his sincerity. There were hushed tones in the lobby and voices murmuring in agreement. "Well, thanks to your, *YOUR* efforts, ladies and gentlemen, the first forty rooms are ready for this first group to move into." There was an eruption of applause from those gathered in the lobby. "Now, for the real hero of the hour, I am going to ask Father Tom O'Hara, to come here and say a few words." The applause was deafening as the tall, slightly slouched priest walked, with the aid of a cane to the microphone.

"*Thank you*, thank you all for your kindness, and the compassion which you have shown this misfortunate community.

"The homeless, men, women, and young adults, who are set to move in later today are just so grateful to everyone for their help in allowing them to build a life, a new life for themselves, away from the harshness of the streets." Father O'Hara slapped his hands together and beamed as he looked around him, he couldn't believe the generosity of those gathered in the hotel. "Now, without any more speeches, you are all more than welcome to join us for a round of coffee and some delicious treats made by our very own Sister Angelica. Thank you, ladies, and gentlemen." He handed the microphone back to John Josess. He smiled warmly at him and walked over to the nuns and led the group over to where several tables had been laid out earlier with coffee and cakes. It all looked so grand, that one could almost be forgiven for thinking it was a reception for the opening of a hotel rather than the opening of a homeless shelter.

Sister Angelica poured a cup of coffee and handed it to John Josess, he took it from the nun, without a word and turned to Father O'Hara and said in a low tone. "The residents will be moving in tonight then?" The priest nodded and looked pleased with himself. He had accomplished so much for the parish.

"Some of the tenants have already begun to put their belongings in their rooms." The priest said smugly. It was evident from his demeanour that he was proud of his parish for the relentless work that they had done to acquire the hotel. It had been no mean feat, either. Their determination had been remarkable, and admirable.

"Aren't they afraid of the reputation of the hotel?" Josess commented and smirked to himself as he took a sip of coffee.

He wanted to stir things up a little, and now was as good a time as any to unsettle the priest.

"These people have lived in worse circumstances than the reputation of these bricks and mortar, Mr Josess." Father Tom O'Hara put his cup down on the table, looked at Josess briefly and then went over to a woman, who was struggling with a trolley. John Josess watched him carefully. He was the embodiment of kindness, and everyone seemed to like him. He had a certain entre nous, and humble with it.

"Thank you, father." She said and smiled brightly, revealing her broken front tooth and the missing teeth from her lower gums. She was a complete mess from years of addiction, and her downtrodden character was etched in her face.

"You are most welcome, my dear." He answered and held the lift doors open as she struggled to move the trolley into the elevator. Tom stood aside and as the doors closed, he wore a self-satisfied smirk once more as one by one, the new residents came into the lobby, in what was now their new home, in the grandest of art deco buildings in this very dilapidated area of LA.

"Couldn't they have waited until we had left?" A refined voice said disdainfully from the crowd. "Filthy pigs, the lot of them." But in the moment that Father O'Hara turned around to confront the naysayer, he was joined by a reporter asking him questions about the project. He nodded and spoke at length with the journalist, but he was perturbed by the outburst, and it showed on his face. *Why couldn't they leave these poor souls alone? Was it really so bad that they be homed in this hotel?*

*****

Father Tom O'Hara walked across the marbled lobby and over to the door, it had been a successful day, and the residents were now installed in their new homes. They were delighted not to be spending another night on the street, afraid, cold and tormented. Tom was happy too, and now that the grand opening was over, he could relax and return to his home and begin writing his sermon for church in the morning. It had been a great day for his parish, for his community. For him, but he should keep his vanity in check, shouldn't he? He thought to himself. Surely God would forgive him, his pride this one time.

"Good night, Father," The concierge called to him as he reached the door. He turned and waved.

"Good night, Hank." He called back and opened the door and walked out into the night air. It was crisp, and a little chilly.

As he looked around and pulled his coat closer to him, he heard the gasps and cries of people on the street, and without warning, a body bounced onto the pavement just feet in front of him. *A suicide!*

Father O'Hara knelt down beside the poor unfortunate body, the face was mashed to a pulp and the way the body lay on the ground he could tell, that the victim had died instantly. He blessed himself and began to pray over the deceased, though prayers were not a comfort for the poor soul, now. Nothing was!

A crowd had gathered around and the sirens in the distance seemed to be taking their time getting to the hotel. There usually was never a rush to get here, jumpers were a regular occurrence. No one seemed to care about these people. In their minds, the residents of skid row were not human, just the embodiment of addiction and human degradation. An embarrassment to be hidden away and ridiculed whenever the occasion arose. Like earlier in the hotel, during the speeches.

Several cops were trying to push back the onlookers, that was now gathering around, straining their necks, rubbernecking to catch a glimpse of the broken and battered body lying on the ground. The ghouls were satisfying their dark curiosity at seeing the twisted remains, with brain and bone hanging out, and nothing remained that resembled a human being anymore.

"Poor sonofabitch." One of the bystanders said as he observed the scene, then added. "What a way to go, probably felt nothing because he was so high." Father O'Hara stared at him, he didn't recognise him, but his words were far from comforting. He was incensed by the callousness of it.

"You couldn't pay me enough to set foot in there, no matter how desperate I was." Another bystander jibed. "Place is haunted. I heard-"

"Please, that kind of talk isn't helpful." The priest cut him off. "Let these poor people grieve without listening to your negative spin." He walked over to one of the new residents and put an arm around her shoulder, she was inconsolable. "There, there, he is at peace now." His words were meant to be a comfort to the woman, but the priest was aware that they were not having the effect he wanted them to have.

"But father, father," the distraught woman cried, her thin fragile frame shook from the enormity of her grief.

"Do you know who it might have been, Grace?" Father O'Hara asked gently, and he kept his arm around her, offering the only comfort that he could. Hearing this, one of the cops came over to them and said gruffly.

"No putting words in the witness's mouth, got it pastor?" The priest looked shocked. This was unbelievable. The insensitivity was astounding to him, even at such a time as this.

"Now, look here," He was getting angry. He had lost too many parishioners lately, and he wasn't in the kind of mood to be told what he could say by way of comfort to one of his flock. He wondered what right the policeman had to dictate how he should console the bereft residents, how dare these people be so cruel?

"Father, go home, let the professionals do their job." The cop grinned at him in a condescending manner and tried to move him on. But the priest was having none of it.

"Father O'Hara," Grace called over to him and he looked at her, he turned quickly and just glared at the cop and then walked over to the woman and held out his arms. "It was Sol, Father O'Hara." She broke down again. The woman was inconsolable, Sol had been Grace's friend.

"Are you sure, Grace?" He asked. He knew Sol was waiting for a room, but he hadn't been on the list of new residents that had gotten rooms. He wondered why he was in the hotel, much less how he had managed to get through the fire escape without setting off any alarms.

"It was *Sol*." She repeated. "It was poor Sol." Tom shook his head from side to side and led her back inside into the hotel to get a cup of coffee and to calm her down.

Chapter 4

Luca Meridian was sitting behind his desk and wore a huge grin as he had just sold five million dollars' worth of cryrocoin. He had been trading in crypto currency for five years, and this was the highest margin that he had made from a single buyer. He was in the mood to celebrate, and to celebrate big.

His phone burst into life, a text had come and he read it. *'Dinner at 9, bikes are finished. Peo.'* He put the phone on his desk. He was looking forward to going out. It had been a while since he had gone out with his friends. They had made plans to go to dinner and then onto Bjorn's nightclub. It was always a good night, with lots to entertain them and lots of distractions. *The nicest kind of distraction!*

Luca sat back in his chair and began to swirl from side to side, he was lost in thought. He had come a long way from where he began in his original career. *A long way indeed!*

The door opened and his secretary came in and said confidently. "There's a gentleman to see you, sir." Luca looked up at her, she was in the job less than six weeks. His PA, whom he depended on, was out on maternity leave. Luca wasn't impressed, not with this girl.

"Who is it?"

"A Mr Demis, sir."

"Send him in," Luca uttered. "I'm not to be disturbed." She left the office and Luca stood up and buttoned his vintage Boss jacket and walked to the centre of the room and waited for Demis. He held out his hand and grinned at him. "Demis, how well you look." His friend looked around the office distastefully and nodded. He wore an expression which always made him look pissed off, Luca was used to him and his eccentricities.

"With all your money, you couldn't brighten this place up, no?" Demis said in a tone that matched his disdainful expression. He began to tut loudly, and Luca just chuckled.

"Can I get you a whiskey?" Luca suggested diplomatically as he walked over to the large drinks' cabinet and motioned to the array of fine whiskies and brandies. He poured a thirty-year-old whiskey into the two glasses.

"I suppose it's a cheap one." Demis said miserably as Luca handed him the crystal glass.

"When do I stock cheap whiskey, Demis?" Luca asked with a smirk. "What has brought you here?" Luca sat down on the large leather sofa and motioned for his friend to sit down too. He knew not to rush him. One never rushed Demis, as he did everything in his own good time.

"You know of all the dimensions you could have chosen, yet you wind up back in this one." Demis exclaimed and took a sip of the whiskey. Luca saw him make a face and laughed. Nothing pleased Demis. He was a disappointed intellectual and wore his failure in academia like a badge on his face. He enjoyed wallowing in his misery, and making those around him, equally as gloomy.

"It's not so bad once you get used to it." Luca reposted, smiling at him as he took a sip of the smooth whiskey.

"I was hoping that the elitist socialite would be here," Demis said as he glanced around the office. He was clearly looking for the others.

"Lanny has a business meeting with an antique dealer." Luca said and grinned as he thought how true, the description of Lanny was. He was an effete snob and never tried to hide it.

"The Praetorian and Berserker, where are they?" He pestered and took a sip of whiskey. His expression barely changed, but Luca could see that he was enjoying the drink. "Doing nothing as usual, I bet." Demis looked at his glass. "Sometimes, I really don't know why I bother."

"I will be meeting all three for dinner, later." Luca revealed as he observed his friend. "You have something to tell me, Demis?" Demis held out the glass to Luca and Luca got up and refilled it. He knew nothing would hurry him and he would only disclose why he visited in his own good time. It was a ceremony in patience, patience that Luca found was running thin with every visit, that the academic made.

Time, tempus! As he remembered it, was of no consequence to Demis. It had no meaning for Luca, either. Or any of them. *Now!*

"The sucker that Lancnut slayed was indeed on a search mission." Demis said as he took the glass from Luca. "The Berserker, is right, they have been summoned to the metropolis and for a reason." He took a sip and Luca sat back down on the sofa and brushed some dust from his thigh.

"Summoned by who?" Luca enquired as he looked at Demis.

"I don't know, how should I?" Demis admitted crankily. "But on my way over, I came across a scene at a hotel. A suicide, was what I heard." Luca stared at him.

"A suicide?" Demis nodded and took another sip. "What hotel?"

"The Cyclades." He spoke gravely. "There was a man of God there. He was very perturbed and as I looked intently at him, I saw his soul in its purity." Luca studied the old philosopher carefully. "It appears that everyone thinks it's a paranormal phenomenon taking place." Luca laughed at this, it amused him to hear of such things and then listen to lengthy explanations as to why it couldn't be. It was a secret pleasure for him, and one he enjoyed thoroughly.

"I know of the Cyclades, and its reputation is deserved." Luca stated. "What has a suicide got to do with us, Demis?"

"I don't know yet, Lucian, but I sense, the soul of the monk is in mystical distress and ripe for the taking if you know what I mean?" Luca laughed loudly. Demis still feared, after all this time.

"Behind all the trappings of your philosophy and theology, Demis, you still fear the dark side." Demis glared at him. "Now you do surprise me."

"I would expect that repost from the Jarl, and anyway my track record has led me to the conclusions that I hold," he said adamantly. "Besides, look whom I have been loaded with to advise." Luca laughed heartily at this, and he knew the old man enjoyed their company, but he would never admit to it.

"And have we not restored your faith, even a little?" Luca was playing with him.

"That's not the point, Lucian." Demis said argumentatively. "I will join you and the others tonight. We'll talk more then." He stood up and handed the glass to Luca. "Until later." He walked over to the door and left. Luca laughed loudly and shook his head.

*****

The restaurant was dimly lit, and the friends were seated near the window, with its splendid view. Luca ordered whiskies for all of them. Peo and Bjorn were deep in conversation when they looked up and saw Demis walk to their table. He looked even more miserable than ever and his clothes more tousled, if it was possible.

"Here comes the life of the party." Lanny said roguishly as he grinned at the others. "Good evening, Demis, how well you look, my friend." Demis snarled a reply but sat down and looked at Lanny who was chuckling at him.

"Jarl, you may have youth on your side," Demis retorted and raised his hand to gain the attention of the waiter. "But this style will never go out of fashion, and fashion is not something I am a slave to." Lanny snorted but before he could reply, Luca asked:

"Do you have an update, Demis?" The philosopher looked sternly at Luca and nodded.

"I followed the monk, at a distance." He said clearly engaged with his news. "There is something negative going on and he's worried for the residents of the hotel." He looked at the others. "I'm not convinced it's paranormal though." Demis said, and he was clearly decided on his opinion.

"What is it then?" Peo inquired as he looked at him. "If it's not paranormal, then what do you want from us?" There was silence for a few minutes as the old intellectual sipped on the whiskey. He wasn't going to be rushed.

"I want you to go to the priest, offer your services," he responded in a serious tone, and he looked at all of them in turn. "Find out what is going on, and who or what is killing the homeless living there." Lanny began to laugh, and they all turned and looked at him, then he shook his head as he leaned on his elbow casually on the table and glanced indifferently around.

"Am I the only one hearing him correctly?" He quizzed. "How can we go to a priest and offer our services?" Luca leaned forward and rested his arms on the table as well. This was going to be interesting.

"He's just another client, what is wrong with helping him?" Luca stated, but he too, was sceptical. Lanny leaned forward and looked at all of them in turn and said in a low tone.

"We're vampires, Luca," he studied him carefully. "A priest, will not accept help from us, he will try to destroy us with his mumbo jumbo." Lanny sat up straight again and he was still shaking his head in disbelief.

"He may not know we're vampires." Bjorn said after a moment, knowingly stoking it with the Jarl. "Not everyone is as astute as you give them credit for, Lanny." Peo agreed with Bjorn. "Besides if someone is killing the homeless, we as Militibus have a duty to help keep them from annihilation by the dregs." He and Lanny locked glances.

"Berserker, I would agree in different circumstances but," Lanny said after a while. "A priest could be detrimental to our health. I for one do not want to have anything to do with a priest." He shrugged his shoulders for effect.

"Always the snob, Lancnut," Demis broke in. "The priest is inherently good. He needs help." Lanny threw his hands up in the air and sighed.

"He could kill us if he chose to." Lanny defended. "With an incantation or an exorcism, or whatever it is a clergyman does."

"No, not unless we give him reason to." Luca contradicted Lanny as he tried hard to hide his grin.

"You are all insane." Lanny protested vehemently. *"Insane!"*

"Ok, Demis, what do we need to do to make contact?" Peo asked and glared at Lanny as he sneered. Peo enjoyed seeing the Jarl in turmoil when no one agreed with him.

"I will insert the thought in his mind, that he needs help with this and to accept your assistance." Demis said in a grave tone. "It's up to you to be in the area, try looking for a place to stay, have a tent pitched down on skid row. The priest will seek you out." Demis said in a casual tone. "He spends his evenings there."

"Skid Row!" Lanny exclaimed loudly. "This gets worse." They all looked at him. "You've lost your mind, Demis." He raved. "This time you've gone too far."

Chapter 5

The tent was difficult to pitch so Peo took over and grinned, Bjorn swore as he inserted the rods awkwardly into the lining of the tent.

"I thought Vikings were expert outdoorsmen." Peo goaded with a sense of humour in the moment. Bjorn glared at him and shook his head, then he unrolled the sleeping bag. He wasn't happy at all, neither of them was pleased with the situation.

"Why do we always get the short straw?" Bjorn grumbled as he took a small flask from inside his jacket. His nose wrinkled as he sniffed the odour from the clothing he was wearing. This was ridiculous, he thought to himself. He was a respectable club owner, and he was reduced to this. It wasn't fair.

"Because we are lowly in rank." Peo said sarcastically but with a slight sense of irritation in his voice also. "Lanny is a Jarl, as we are always reminded." He smirked as he fixed the tent on to the ground, it was lobsided. "Luca is the General after all, our *master*." Bjorn snorted at that. Peo was clearly as pissed off as he was. Neither of them was relishing the night ahead, sleeping rough.

"And what are our roles? What are they without us?" Bjorn grumbled as he fumbled with the bag. "I'll tell you, without us the Jarl and the General would have to get their hands dirty, once in a while." He handed the flask to Peo, and they both laughed. They would have to get into the role of being vagrants. Starting with their complaints about their situation, as they saw it.

They were always grumbling when they had to do work that seemed beneath them. That was when they became uncannily like Lanny, snobbish. But mostly, as a team, the Militibus, were unstoppable. This was the first time though, that they had to go undercover as rough sleepers.

They settled down on the ripped coats that they had folded up and placed on the ground. Peo handed the expensive vintage bottle of wine, that was wrapped in a wrinkled brown bag, to his friend. He sighed, as he remembered he had forgotten to pack some wine glasses.

The night was a little chilly and as they sat on the ground, Bjorn glanced over at the sewer cover near the pavement where they sat. There was steam coming from it. His nose was sensitive, and he could smell the rot coming from the drain. It was rank and disgusting, and it smelled of death. A fresh kill.

"What is it, Bjorn?" Peo asked as he followed his friend's gaze across to the manhole. The steam filled the air.

"I don't know." Bjorn replied but before he could say anything else he heard the voice of the monk coming from a few tents away. "The priest is here." Bjorn nodded at Peo, who looked in the direction that Bjorn had indicated. They watched him stand and talk with the residents and then they heard them laugh. It was difficult for the Militibus to comprehend their mirth given the dire circumstances they found themselves in. But they were upbeat and enjoyed the banter with the padre.

Silently they waited as the priest came slowly along and seemed to stop at every tent to have a word with the occupants. Bjorn could smell him. He could smell the blood coursing through his veins. His heart pounding fast, it seemed irregular as if he struggled with the present. Through it all, Bjorn could sense his goodness and his despair, all at once.

This was the first time that Bjorn had felt this. He felt the priest's sorrow as he engaged in conversation with the people of skid row. He genuinely cared about them. Cared what happened to these forgotten mortals.

"Well, hello there." The priest said to them kindly and held out his hand to Bjorn and then to Peo. "I'm Father Tom O'Hara. I don't believe I met either of you before." He glanced from Bjorn to Peo and smiled. It was a smile full of warmth, comfort and understanding. Sincerity.

"We just got into town." Peo spoke trying to sound broken, but he didn't look the priest in the eyes, he couldn't.

"Where are you from, my son?" Father O'Hara queried gently as he looked from one to the other.

"Out of town." Bjorn replied quickly and lowered his eyes. He didn't want the priest to read the look in his eyes. He feared him. He now, understood what Lanny feared. It was his goodness. Bjorn knew that he was in the company of a man who could out them for what they were, if he looked in their eyes, into their being.

"Have you eaten today?" He asked both of them, gently. They shook their heads and wearily glanced at each other as the priest held out his hand to them and they stood up. Standing next to the priest, both Peo and Bjorn dwarfed him, at six foot four. "Come with me. We don't have a great choice of food but it's warm and wholesome." He said and the Militibus followed him across the road to the soup kitchen, every now and then they glanced at each other, not knowing what to say or how to react.

There were two long industrial style tables with a few men and women sitting at them. They were dipping chunks of bread into thick homemade soup. It smelt good despite being in a soup kitchen.

"Ask Sister Angelica for some sustenance and stay here for as long as it takes to warm up." He said kindly and as he turned to leave, and Bjorn called to him.

"How long have you been doing this?" Father O'Hara turned around and smiled sincerely at him. He could see the aura which surrounded him. It was bright and reflected the goodness in his spirit.

"Since I was called by the Lord, young man." Father O'Hara said sincerely and walked back over to him. "I answered when *He* said he needed me." Bjorn stood up straight. He knew from the past, that good men like this priest existed but he had never met any. Until now. He was impressed by his resilience to do good, despite the backdrop of adversity.

"The building, where the people reside," Bjorn said. "I heard someone say you are responsible for that?" The priest nodded. "Why are the people living on the street in tents, when the building is available?" The priest carefully led him over to the table and motioned him to sit down. His smile had lost some of its warmth and Bjorn could feel his struggle. He was coming close to crisis, not just of his faith but for those on the street that he was trying to help. He felt the clergyman's doubt seep in.

"The hotel has had a bad reputation. Bad things happened there." He said in a sombre voice. "And some of my parishioners listen to talk, and the talk has been of a frightening nature. They are scared." Father O'Hara said and clasped his hands together as if he were praying. "I can understand their reluctance, of course, but I am at my wits end to assure them they are safe inside the hotel, instead of being out on the street." Bjorn looked at him intently, his heartbeat was beginning to slow again to a normal rhythm.

Peo joined them at the table and looked at the priest then to Bjorn. Their eyes met and they both nodded. They knew that they had to get inside the building, but they were unsure of how.

"What have they said?" Peo asked and the priest looked at him with a serious expression. He shook his head from side to side.

"It's just talk," he replied after a moment. "Some have said they have seen ghosts of those who resided there before. I know, it's absurd but these people have battled with their addiction, and some have paranoia, and so they believe what they believe." He nodded to himself.

"Padre, can we go into the hotel?" Peo asked abruptly, much to the annoyance of Bjorn, who just glared at him, he was sometimes just like Lanny, blurting out without thinking first.

"Young man, there is a waiting list for a room." He sighed audibly. "The rooms are finished, of course, but there's red tape, bureaucracy to get through." He hankered. Bjorn sensed his frustration.

"Father O'Hara, is there something that we could do to help?" Bjorn asked sincerely. He didn't know why but this man was influencing him, somehow. In a good way. Almost as if his goodness was like a disease, infectious. He wanted to help, he needed to help any way that he could.

"Son, it is I who should be trying to help both of you." The priest said solemnly as he stood up and then gave a weak smile and looked at them. "Let me see what I can do about getting you a room, but I can't promise anything tonight." Then he turned and walked away but stopped in his tracks and sniffed the air. Bjorn knew at that moment he sensed their scent. Father O'Hara walked over to the door, shaking his head and Bjorn wondered if he was tuned into his gift yet. Did he know that they were vampires, creatures of the night?

"What do you think he's going to do?" Peo asked in a hushed tone. Bjorn turned back to look at the door.

"I think he knows what we are and that something is up." Bjorn uttered and then looked at Peo. "We need to get inside the hotel, tonight, see what we can find." Peo nodded and they both got up and left the hall.

They would wait until late and then go around the back. It would be difficult, but they knew that they had to get inside the hotel.

Chapter 6

The Militibus were sitting in Lanny's penthouse discussing the hotel. Luca was standing over at the window. The lights of the city were glowing, lit up almost like daytime. It was another world when night fell. Full of the weird and wonderful.

"The priest, has a gift." Bjorn said outright and stood up.

"What kind of gift?" Luca asked, still with his back to them. He was enjoying the view from the Jarl's penthouse.

"*He* can smell us." Bjorn said. Lanny laughed loudly as he shook his head and glanced across at Bjorn as he smirked.

"Great, just what we need, a monk with a gift to sniff out vampires." It was no secret that he didn't want to do this job. Lanny hadn't stopped protesting since they took on the assignment. "Just great."

"Do you know if he knows you and Peo are vampires?" Luca questioned, ignoring Lanny's complaints as he turned around. Bjorn shook his head. "We need to invite him to the office. Did you get the impression that he was a sceptic?"

"A sceptic? Really General?" Lanny asked and chuckled. "He's a man of faith, a faith which condemns creatures like us." He walked over to the table and picked up his glass of full-bodied red wine. He took a sip and closed his eyes briefly. Clara had shown him how to saviour wine. *Ah sweet Clara!*

"Bjorn says he can smell, it's not the same as knowing." Luca retorted, a little irritated as he took out his phone. A few moments later the call was answered. "Father O'Hara, you don't know me, my name is Luca Meridian. I understand your parish is seeking funding for your housing project?" He paused and glanced across at his officers. "Can we meet now? To discuss it? Very good. Yes, I know where that is. My colleague and I will see you in half an hour." He hung up and stared at Lanny for a moment, but he simply grinned back and shook his head.

"*No way*...I am not going." Lanny said. "This is suicide to us." He was adamant about it.

"Lanny, grab your cheque book and let's go, we have an engagement with the priest." Luca ordered and turned to the other two and spoke firmly. "Get back to your posts on skid row. Find out what you can from the others living there." He ordered and grinned across at Lanny.

Lanny and Luca walked purposefully along the street and stopped outside the old iron gate. Luca looked at Lanny briefly and then pushed open the gate and they walked up the steps to the parochial house. Luca rang the bell and turned his back to the door and waited, it was a balmy night.

A few minutes later the door opened and a kindly old woman, a little hunched over greeted them warmly, and stood aside and welcomed them. But Lanny and Luca just waited, and the old lady laughed heartily and said with a grin. "Where are my manners, gentlemen, please do come in." They nodded at her and followed her into the library.

Lanny walked over to the bookcase. He cast an expert eye over the rows of leather-bound books. He was impressed. "For a clergyman, he has a fine collection." Lanny commented in a serious tone as he thumbed through the book which he held in his hand.

"For a clergyman, I read more than just the bible." A friendly voice chuckled from the doorway. Lanny turned as the priest came into the room, smiling. "Do you read books young man?" He asked glancing up at Lanny, who regarded him with uncertainty. He didn't look threatening, and Lanny sensed what the others sensed around the priest, righteousness.

"Yes, of course I do, why do you ask?" Lanny said coolly. "I have a keen interest in philosophy." Father O'Hara nodded, he seemed impressed, but Lanny didn't care. He wasn't there to make friends and certainly not to make friends with a man of the cloth.

"A conversation, I would love to have with you, young man." He articulated warmly.

"My name is Lanny." He said emotionless as he eyed the clergyman carefully. "Lanny Lancnut." The priest held out his hand and a little reluctantly Lanny shook it. A look flashed in his eyes and Lanny saw it. The priest had immediately seen what Lanny was and he was fearful as he tried to disguise it.

"I'm Luca Meridian." Luca said and held out his hand too. The priest shook it.

"My but you both have a strong shake." He said a little tautly and Lanny sensed he was trying to figure out what had happened, he was on heightened alert. Nervous!

"You know what we are, don't you?" Lanny stated abruptly and stood up to his full height of six foot seven. The clergyman glanced at him and blessed himself. Lanny smiled at this, he was amused now, and he wanted to have fun with him. Upset him even.

"Father O'Hara," Luca said as he came forward to him. "We are here to help." He quickly looked at Lanny and then to the priest. The Jarl could see that Luca was also wary of the situation now.

"Oh god help me, but I don't need your kind of help." The priest said, panicked and fearful.

"Our kind of help?" Lanny queried angrily as he glared at him. "What kind of assistance do you think we are offering?" He asked forcefully now.

"I know what you are." Father O'Hara answered quickly and reached into his shirt and took out a cross. Lanny laughed loudly at this.

"You think brandishing that piece of jewellery, works?" Lanny asked spiritedly and smiled as he walked toward the man. "No padre, it doesn't work." Lanny wanted to play with him some more, to prey on his fear. It would give him perverted pleasure.

"You are an evil, get out." The old priest cried and backed slowly away from the vampire. "Dear God in heaven, protect me from the evil standing before me, I pray to you oh God." Lanny snorted as he looked at him and stepped closer to the priest.

"Lanny, quit your game." Luca said insistently and walked over to the chair which was beside the fireplace and sat down. "Father O'Hara please sit down." He motioned to the chair on the other side of the fire. The old man did as he was told, he was fearful for his life. "We're not here to hurt you. We're here to help." Luca repeated and watched as Lanny walked over to the bookcase and began to examine the rows of books again. "Tell us about the hotel, what's been happening there?" Luca coaxed him gently and glanced across at the Jarl.

"Aristotle," Lanny exulted suddenly and held up a yellowed leather book. "Demis wouldn't be happy." He snickered and put the book back and walked over to the sofa and sat down and looked intently at the priest. He was enjoying tormenting the cleric and seeing his fear as he dared to look back over at the vampire.

"You know about the hotel?" Father O'Hara asked cautiously, and they both nodded. "Well, about a month ago, on the day it opened. There was a suicide, Sol, a terrible paranoid drunk, he jumped to his death from the seventh floor. Then for seven nights a resident jumped from various floors, floors which weren't occupied, still aren't. The police weren't helpful either because those poor souls were from skid row." He shook his head gravely. The man looked helpless as if he blamed himself, for somehow not being able to prevent it.

"The hotel has been known to house serial killers and violent criminals in the past." Lanny said carelessly and crossed his leg. "Was it such a surprise about the jumpers?" Father O'Hara leaned back in the armchair and sighed, it was clear he was distressed.

"God help me, I am speaking with devils." He muttered and blessed himself again and began to mumble a prayer.

"Vampires, are the undead." Lanny corrected him with a smirk on his handsome face. "We're not devils, that's another group of dregs altogether. Now go on." He smiled at the tortured man.

"Surprisingly as a man of faith, I don't believe that ghosts are killing innocent people." He looked across at Lanny as if trying to convince himself he was hallucinating. "I think what is happening is to do with the living and not the dead." He looked at Lanny. "No offence." Lanny shook his head and grinned at him.

"None taken." Lanny said simpering. "Why would a living soul want to kill the residents?"

"I don't know. These unfortunate people have been through so much pain." Tom O'Hara spoke. "Why indeed." His hands were clasped together and rested on his rounded stomach.

"We will need access to the hotel, to see what is going on inside." Luca said in a serious note after a moment. "We have two men there already, keeping an eye on the place, as we speak." He looked at the priest reassuringly.

"Ah, the two newcomers." Father O'Hara said after a moment. "They are like both of you. I sensed it." He scratched his balding head. He appeared confused. "They seem nice boys. Decent."

"We are not what you think we are," Luca reiterated in a calm tone. "We help people like you. Good people that need assistance with bad individuals that wish to harm them." It was the priest's turn to laugh now. Both Lanny and Luca stared at him incredulously.

"Vampires doing good?" He chuckled. "Don't you suck the life blood from your victims and let them die agonisingly." He looked from one to the other disbelievingly that he was conversing with the undead.

"For a man with a library extensively stocked as yours is." Lanny said as he stood up. "You have absolutely no idea about our kind, as you put it." Luca stood up as well and held out his hand.

"We'll be in touch, Father." He said and glared at Lanny to shake hands with the old man. He did. "Rest assured, whatever or whoever is behind this, we will get to the bottom of it." Luca looked at him reassuringly.

"Your soul won't be damaged by it either, padre." Lanny said and grinned as he walked over to the door and opened it. "Good evening." He said in as deep a voice as he could muster and laughed as they closed the door behind them.

"Really Lanny, that was very immature." Luca scolded, but the sides of his mouth were hiding the grin, that he supressed, and Lanny laughed raucously as they walked over to the car, got in and drove away.

Chapter 7

Peo pulled the collar of his coat up around his neck, he had been sitting with his back to the wall for the last hour or so. His butt was numb, and he was in a seriously pissed off mood. He hoped that none of his customers would come to this disreputable part of town and see him sitting as a homeless person on skid row. His reputation as an antique weapons dealer would be ruined. *Forever!*

He moved his head from side to side. He was stiff and wanted a nice juicy, very rare fillet steak with a full-bodied red wine, or a single malt whiskey.

Peo wondered what kept Bjorn, he had said that he was going to get them some coffee. Thinking about coffee, Peo thought to himself that he would prefer something a little stronger. A brandy to provide some warmth, and maybe a mortal woman or two. *Definitely some female company.*

He stared down the alley as there was a commotion which seemed to be getting louder. Peo saw two men harassing a woman. Peo sniffed the air. *Suckers!*

He stood up, and as he did, Bjorn came up to him and handed him a cardboard cup of coffee. "Suckers!" Peo said as he took the hot drink from Bjorn. They both looked down the alleyway at the scene as it progressed.

"Leave it." Bjorn told him as he observed the scene. "Unless they come to us." Peo was about to say something but before he could, Bjorn's demeanour changed and he had stood up straight and with his right hand he reached for the handle of his mace, from inside his coat. They were always ready to defend themselves.

A tall man wearing a denim jacket and black jeans, strolled over to them, from his stagger, they could tell that he was intoxicated from the blood that he had drunk. He could hardly stand, let alone walk.

Peo stood up straight, with his legs spread apart. He was ready to attack if necessary. Some action would be welcome, to liven up the monotony of the night. He would welcome it.

"Well, well, well." The street vampire said as he looked from side to side at Peo and Bjorn. "What do we have here?" He sneered as he reached out to touch Bjorn's dirty jacket. The man was now joined by the other sucker who sniggered as he looked them up and down. Peo could see the blood trickling down his chin. It disgusted him to be that close to dregs.

"Move on suckers and we won't send you to hell." Peo warned as his hand gripped the handle of his sword. He hated these monsters.

The two creatures laughed as they looked at each other. "He won't send us to hell." The first sucker said and grinned as he grabbed Peo by the jacket. Peo's nose twitched at the smell of the vampire's bloodied breath. "You elitist snob." He growled at Peo when he saw his reaction. "I say we send you to hell, Militibus."

"Back away." Peo cautioned once more. "I won't tell you again." The two suckers laughed at this.

Without warning, Peo drew his sword and lashed out, the parasite's head went flying into the air and then dropped at the feet of the second one. Peo turned in a three sixty and swung his sword at the second sucker's neck, but it didn't quite sever completely. He swore when he saw it, barely holding on by the thin black sinewy veins.

Bjorn snorted loudly and tugged at the head, and it gave way. "Losing your touch, Praetorian." He jibed as they picked up the two heads and threw them on top of the predators' bodies. They stepped away as a bright light consumed the remains and in a matter of minutes all that remained was a pile of black dust.

They both snickered and high fived each other.

Peo and Bjorn stood up straight and Peo took a rag from his pocket and wiped the black slime from the blade of his sword. As he glanced down the alley, he saw a few homeless people had gathered and were muttering amongst themselves. They were pointing at Peo, and he saw that they were scared, and he couldn't blame them. They must have thought they were hallucinating.

"This isn't good." Peo observed as he sheathed his sword. "We better leave. Call the General." Bjorn took out his phone and called Luca as they walked away. This had gone south and quickly.

*****

"Three bloodsuckers in as many nights." Luca recalled with concern as he looked at Bjorn and Peo. "There were no suckers left after the last battle over three years ago." He eyed both of them and then began to pace up and down. It wasn't good. "Why now?"

"A few drunks saw it happen." Peo confessed reluctantly. "This could be problematic." He looked worried too.

"The cops won't believe anything from a few men who reek of cheap alcohol." Lanny scoffed as he grinned at them. "You forget, Praetorian, they are the forgotten people, the unwanted." They knew he was right, despite the sarcasm.

"Lanny, since we began the surveillance at the hotel," Peo said as he looked at him intently. "They have been sober, in the main, from what we have seen." Somehow, he needed to let the Jarl and the General know this. It seemed important for the sake of the residents, at least.

"Word on skid row is if you want a room, you have to be sober." Bjorn offered in support of his friend.

"Once a drunk..." Lanny mumbled but didn't finish it. He was being unfair, and he knew it.

Everyone in the room knew that he didn't want this job because he felt superior to those that he was protecting. It was just how the Jarl was. They accepted that he would never change.

Luca stopped pacing and began to stroke his chin thoughtfully. "How many suckers were in the group you encountered, Lanny?" He asked him casually.

"Three." Lanny replied with a bored attitude.

Luca was perturbed by the fact that there were dregs coming back into the city. He didn't like them hanging around. "Return to your posts. Lanny and I will join you shortly." Peo and Bjorn nodded and walked over to the door and left.

Lanny watched as the door closed, then he turned to Luca and asked in a stern tone. "What do think is going on, General?" Luca just looked at him for a moment. "Something has brought them into the city."

"I agree and I also think there is a lair in the city's sewers," Lanny looked at him. "And it's expanding."

"After all this time?" Lanny queried. "Why now?"

"I'm not sure why but we will find out." Luca said as he looked at his second in command. "Let's go." The two vampires left the penthouse.

Chapter 8

Lanny jumped off the back of the panigale. He removed his helmet and placed it onto the seat of the powerful machine. He sniffed the air and looked with disdain at the rows of tents in the distance. He hated this part of town. It was filthy.

He saw steam rising from the sewers. Lanny reached inside the pocket of his long black leather coat. He felt the handle of the axe on his left side, his sword was in its scabbard to his right. He was always prepared to fight.

"Looks quiet." Luca observed as he walked over to where Lanny stood, he nodded. Lanny looked up at the Cyclades hotel. There were a few lights illuminating various windows on the third to sixth floors. The seventh floor was in complete darkness.

"I thought all floors to the seventh, were occupied?" Lanny questioned as they both looked up. It didn't appear to be the case. Something wasn't right.

"There are only a couple of rooms on six and seven, with residents." Luca replied and Lanny observed as Luca put his hand on the handle of his sword.

"Are you expecting trouble, General?" He asked with a slight grin as they began to walk. The two Militibus cut dashing yet frightening figures as they walked. They looked out of place down on skid row.

As they crossed the road, Lanny saw Peo and Bjorn stand up as they approached. He glanced around at the squalor. The stench in the air, which had nothing to do with tent city, but it was an assault to his sensitive nose. He couldn't wait to leave.

"What is it?" Bjorn asked as he saw Lanny's expression.

"I'm not sure." Lanny replied as he glanced around. "How long has that smell been in the air?" Bjorn looked around too and then stood up straight as he stood next to the Jarl. The Vikings were alert.

"I noticed it the first night we came down here." Bjorn said and then asked. "What could it be?" The Jarl wasn't sure, but it could be bloodsuckers.

"I think it's a lair." Lanny replied almost to himself as he looked around again and reached for his axe.

"Be careful with the weapons, Lanny." Peo said with a warning tone. "Everyone here seems restless tonight and there have already been three black and whites patrolling in the last hour alone." Lanny nodded and removed his hand from the handle of the axe.

"Lanny and I will go investigate the hotel." Luca spoke and then added. "Be vigilant." They nodded their agreement.

Luca and Lanny moved with caution over to the door of the hotel. Luca tried the handle, and it opened. Noiselessly, they moved very quickly, and slipped inside unnoticed.

On the stairwell, and hidden away from the reception desk, Luca pointed upstairs. Lanny nodded and at the top, they separated and went off silently in different directions.

Lanny had his hand on the handle of his axe, as he walked along the corridor of the third floor. He listened to the sounds of life inside the apartments as he passed each door. In some of the rooms, he could hear a radio, or a television on. He could also hear the heartbeats and the blood flow of the residents inside. Normal activity, nothing unusual.

Even though they had fed a few months ago, Lanny always felt a pang when he heard the flow of blood. He had first felt the hunger pain as it stabbed his stomach, after the raid on Lindisfarne, when he was turned, and again when they arrived and raided Wessex, just before his mortal body died and his vampire appetite took over. A craving, he never knew could be so painful and so insistent.

After he had returned to Lasgard, when they had sacked the village in Wessex, Lanny was banished but his thirst grew even more fierce, and he was unable to control the need to feed. That was when he first met Demis and Luca. It was Demis who had crudely forced him through the portal. It had been closing fast, and he had pushed Lanny so hard, that he threw up with the strength of the g-forces that enveloped him. Demis had enjoyed that. *Miserable old toad that he was!*

When it had stopped, Luca had laughed hysterically and then handed him a towel to wipe the vomit from his face and chest and then they took him to the hospital to be drained of the poisonous alpha vampire blood and to have the new, Militibus blood fed to him intravenously, it would be the only way he would feed in future.

What was that? Lanny sniffed. *Sucker!*

Lanny removed his axe and unsheathed his broad sword from inside his long leather coat carefully, and silently made his way down the darkened corridor.

He heard the whimpers of a man and then weakening grunts. Lanny knew only too well what it was, the sucker was torturing the man, before death took him. He glanced around the corner, the light from the ceiling began to flicker, signalling his presence, and he could see the frightened look on the man's face as his tormentor was licking his face with a thick blood covered tongue. Fear filled the air with its foul stench. There was something else too, and he needed to control his lust for it. It's aroma, saturated the air with its thick smell.

"Ahh, it seems we have company." The street vampire said as he turned his head and laughed when he saw Lanny. "Get out of here, asshole, and find your own meal." Lanny walked slowly into the centre of the hallway, flicking the axe in his hand, ready for action. He stood tall and impressive, in his leathers and his long blond hair flowing loose down his back, his steel blue eyes glared back at the other vampire.

"Let him go." Lanny ordered in a firm voice. "Let him go, and I won't kill you." Although there was nothing that would save the victim now, his mortal body was almost dead, thanks to the bleeding from his jugular, caused by the bloodsucker. This made the sucker laugh as he turned to look at Lanny. He could see the traces of blood trickling from the side of his mouth, and down onto his chin. Fresh human blood. Warm red blood. Lanny could almost taste it.

"How about I kill both of you instead?" The sucker said as he glanced at the unfortunate victim, whose throat he had almost crushed by his hand.

"I wouldn't count on you winning against me, sucker." Lanny said confidently as he walked closer to the parasite, who was still laughing as he held the mortal at arm's length.

"You are mistaken," he said grinning and without warning ran at the window and threw the unfortunate man forcefully breaking the glass and the wooden frame as the battered body connected with the window and fell to his death. Death being an ease to him when it finally came, on impact with the concrete below.

Lanny gave a lobsided half smile as he swayed the axe and sword together in his hands, in a three sixty and lashed out at the criminal. He extended the axe and plunged it at the vampire's chest. The sucker looked at the tear on his t-shirt and then at Lanny and snorted as he moved carefully in a circle. "You missed." Lanny smirked at him and shook his head, his expression cold and hard.

"You think I missed?" Lanny goaded as he swung around, his long legs firmly apart as he stared at him, and stretched his axe and connected it at the sucker's neck. "I never miss, sucker." The vampire fell to his knees and held his hand to his neck, where the dark sticky goo, oozed from the wound. Lanny stood over him. "Where's the lair?" The sucker laughed, as blood spewed over his hand from the cut on his neck. Lanny heard the gurgle, but he was careful not to sever the head from the body until he had the information he wanted.

"I'm not telling you, anything asshole." He said sneering. "But I will tell you this, there are more than you can handle, Militibus." He was laughing uncontrollably now.

"Requiem in inferno." Lanny shouted as he stood over him and with his axe raised, he swiped the head cleanly from the body. The head rolled and fell at his boots. Lanny groaned loudly. This displeased him as he kicked it back to the body and stepped backwards as the vampire turned to a heap of black powder on the ground.

Lanny walked over to the broken window frame and glanced down onto the street below. He saw the twisted corpse lying on the ground, a few people were gathered around the body. It was better for the human, that he had died first. As he turned to walk away, Lanny looked up and he saw Luca running toward him. He stopped and looked at the pile of dust on the ground and then at Lanny.

"What happened?" Luca asked.

"He was torturing the victim," Lanny said emotionless. "He flung him out of the window, so I sent him to the Tenth." Luca walked over to the window and looked out.

"That's unfortunate." Luca said dispassionately and walked over to Lanny. "Did he say anything?"

"There is a lair, but he refused to say where." Lanny said. "We should check the sewers it might be there." Luca nodded and they hurriedly retreated back the way that they had come.

Back outside on the street, they ran over to where the Praetorian and the Berserker had kept watch, they heard the sirens, Luca motioned for them to get to the bikes and the four Militibus hurriedly left the scene.

Chapter 9

Father Tom O'Hara handed a glass each to the two men that were sitting in the library. He then walked back over to the oak cabinet and picked up his own glass of sherry, then walked back over to the armchair beside the large fireplace and sat down. He glanced at them as he took a sip.

"Your health, O'Hara." The older man raised a glass in a toasting gesture to Father O'Hara. "Tell me, how is the cause coming along?" The older man asked in a sarcastic tone as he raised the glass to his mouth and took a sip and made a face.

"Of course there's some hiccups," Father O'Hara admitted. "But I am confident that these will iron themselves out by the time the next group of residents move in." He took a sip of the dry sherry. It was a pleasure that he allowed himself to indulge regularly. He usually enjoyed it but not now, not like this when he was worried about the project failing.

"There have been five more suicides, I understand." John Josess inferred in a matter-of-fact tone. "There has been rumour around the committee offices, that the homeless are refusing to move into the hotel, some nonsense about ghosts and killers lopping off heads." This had disturbed the priest too when he spoke with a representative from the homeless group awaiting the keys to their rooms. The recipients were refusing to move from the street. It was understandable but it was giving him an ulcer.

"Naturally," Father O'Hara said hesitantly. "There is an apprehension on their part to move in, but these people are somewhat superstitious anyway and given the past reputation the hotel had, it isn't easy to convince them otherwise." He nervously took another sip from his glass, and his hand tremored a little. He was on edge, and it was taking its toll on him.

"They are an ungrateful lot." The other man said from across the room. "Considering what you have done to get this project off the ground. You're to be commended O'Hara or committed." There was no sincerity in the man's voice or his demeanour. Father O'Hara glanced across at the man. He didn't take to compliments of this nature. It was his calling to help his flock, he wasn't exceptional, he just cared. He was empathetic that was all, nothing more than that.

He stood up and took the sherry glasses from his visitors and went back to the cabinet and refilled them and then handed them back to his guests once more. They both made a face. It was beneath their tastes and pallet.

"These people haven't had it easy." Father O'Hara went on, trying to convince them, as he sat down once more. "I'm not doing this for gratitude." He looked at the two men. "I'm doing it because I'm their last hope." Their only hope, he thought sadly.

"A noble cause in your book, Father O'Hara, brownie points with your boss upstairs, huh." Josess said in a snarky voice and put his glass on the coffee table. "Still, a little appreciation would be good considering the hotel is prime real estate, wouldn't you agree, Frank?" He turned to his companion, who stood up and sneered as he looked at the priest. He looked as if he wore a permanent smirk on his face.

"Thank you for your hospitality, O'Hara." Frank said and walked to the library door, he paused for a moment. "If the drunks refuse to move into their new homes, as they are ready. I'll have to reconsider the purpose of the hotel." He left the room followed by Father O'Hara and John Josess. This was not what Tom needed to hear right now. This was disastrous news, for all concerned.

"I assure you, the residents will move in, you have my word on that." Father O'Hara said quickly. "We just need a little patience." He would have to convince them. *Somehow!*

"No," Frank said with a mordant expression. "If they refuse to move in, I will repurpose the use of the hotel." He opened the front door and left, chased by Josess.

Father O'Hara stood on the step staring helplessly after them. This was not good at all. What would he do if they refused to move in? He just hadn't thought about that. Tom shook his head despondently.

He closed the door and walked back into the library. He felt defeated. He knew that both Josess and Frank Rostern meant what they said about repurposing the building. They were businessmen, and they were ruthless men. He knew that they were only interested in making money, there was no charity in those men whatsoever. But wasn't he, Tom being uncharitable now, questioning their kindness?

He sat back in the armchair and his thoughts turned to the visit he had had a few weeks before from the two...men. He didn't want to think about them. Father O'Hara wondered what his bishop would say if he knew that he had put his fate in the hands of two vampires. *Dear God, help him, but he was working too hard!*

The doorbell rang and he heard the muffled voices in the hall, then the library door opened, and his housekeeper came in.

"Two gentlemen to see you, Father." She said cheerily and from the look on her face, he knew who it was.

"Show them in." He forced a smile and stood up as the door opened wide and he saw the two vampires walk into the library. He looked at them briefly. They were immaculately dressed and groomed, as they had been previously, wearing expensive suits. "What can I do for you two...gentlemen?" The priest asked, he was perturbed by their presence again.

"Good evening, padre." The blond man said with a grin, and he came into the room and walked over to the armchair and without waiting to be asked, he arrogantly sat down. He didn't take his eyes off Tom. He was an intense...man!

"What...what can I do for you?" Tom O'Hara asked hesitantly, as he looked at him.

"Lanny," the blond vampire informed Tom and smiled at him, revealing perfectly white teeth. "We've come from the Cyclades." He said in a deep accented baritone voice. He would be a very dashing looking man, if he had been human, so self-assured, so confident, Father O'Hara thought to himself and then he shook his head. He had to stop thinking like this. The man was a monster.

"Oh," Father O'Hara said as he motioned to the other vampire to sit down. He himself, sat down on the sofa and gave them his fullest attention, he really had little choice.

"There was a murder there, two nights ago." The dark-haired man said gravely. This disturbed the priest even further.

"Murder?" Tom asked, not sure he had heard correctly. "But it has been reported as a suicide by the witnesses. The residents were so upset by it." He scratched his head now. Confused.

"It was murder, I can confirm it." Lanny said with a half-smile. "I observed it happen." Father O'Hara suddenly stared at him. Was he involved? Probably!

"You witnessed it?" He repeated, Lanny nodded. "Ho...how?"

"The General and I went to check out the building, as we agreed with you," he said in a serious tone now. "There was a vampire harrying the victim, then he threw him through the window."

"A vampire? Like you?" Father O'Hara asked him incredulously. He was stunned.

"I am not a blood addicted sucker." Lanny said indignantly. "I don't kill to drink blood." He could see that the vampire was angry, and he didn't want to incense him further. He just wanted them to leave him alone. *Why won't they leave me alone?* He thought to himself.

"What Lanny means," Luca interjected. "Some vampires are not as gracious or cordial like the Tempus Militibus." Father O'Hara rubbed his cheeks with his hands. He was afraid now.

"This is a terrible distressing situation." He said and looked at the blond vampire again. "The police found only poor Vincent's broken body. There was no one else."

"That's because I beheaded the sucker and he crumbled into dust." Lanny said without mincing his words. Tom shuddered.

"Dear God, you killed him?" Father O'Hara asked, in a despairing tone.

"No, I sent him back to the Tenth dimension." Lanny corrected him and grinned. Father O'Hara got the feeling that the vampire was enjoying his predicament and his fear.

"What dimension?" The priest was confused, and his temples were beginning to pound with a headache. He needed an aspirin and an early night.

"It's where the vilest of souls are imprisoned." Lanny said, there was a slight irritation in his voice. "When a dreg does something bad, their energy is imprisoned in the Tenth dimension. Never to be released." Lanny said, his voice a little less harsh now than it had been.

"I don't understand." Father O'Hara said. None of this was making any sense to him. He was not a man of science; he was only a man of faith.

"For all your theological teachings, you don't grasp the basics of crime and punishment?" Lanny asked amused as he looked at him. The intensity of the man was disturbing Tom.

"Of course, I do, it's just the idea of souls trapped without even trying for redemption or some kind of salvation is beyond me." Father O'Hara said quarrelsomely and stood up. He believed in redemption and forgiveness. For all!

"Save your prayers for the souls you can save." Lanny said cynically as Father O'Hara looked at him.

"You don't believe in rehabilitation of those who lose their way?" Father O'Hara asked the vampire. "What about your soul? What have you done to save it?" He looked across at the blond, and he saw him grinning.

"I have done no wrong since I was turned, padre." Lanny argued bitterly. "I was wronged when I was turned." His look was even more intense and seemed to bore right through him. Tom felt his grievance at his situation.

"Can we tend to the matter at hand and save the theology discussion for another time, Jarl." Luca interrupted and Tom saw the look which passed between the two vampires. He wondered about their association.

"Of course, Mr..."

"Luca Meridian." Luca replied. "The residents of the hotel seem terrified by the building. Have you spoken with any of them, Father O'Hara?"

"Yes, they are convinced the goings on there are supernatural in nature." He replied, distressed. "It is, in a manner of speaking, isn't it? There is nothing I can do to alleviate their fears." He was desperate as he looked fearfully at his two visitors.

"We will have the Praetorian and the Berserker talk to those living there and find out if they have seen any suckers prior to their moving in." Lanny interposed as he stood up and held out his hand to him. Tom shook it but was taken aback by the heat from his skin. "Yes, my skin is warm because I have blood pumping through my veins, padre." His smile was beautiful. He was a beautiful looking man, they both were, Father O'Hara thought as he looked at the vampires, really looked at them. They resembled human men, not the supernatural beings that they were. That monstrous reputation that the creatures of the night had.

"We will be in touch soon, Father O'Hara," Luca said and shook hands with him. "For now, please do not discuss this with anyone else." He warned. "It would be very unhelpful to us if you did."

"Of course." Father O'Hara agreed. He didn't want to let on to anyone, that he was talking to vampires. He feared his bishop would have him committed if he did. He would be justified too.

"Good evening," Lanny said with a grin as he looked at him, and Tom sensed that the blond vampire had a good sense of humour and liked to shock him. He thought his reaction must be a source of entertainment, particularly for the vampire, Lanny. He waved at them as he led them out of the parochial house.

Chapter 10

Luca leaned back against the plush leather armchair. He felt relaxed and he was enjoying the smooth strains of the piano coming from the top of the range stereo. He had just poured himself a glass of one hundred- and twenty-year-old Midleton whisky, it partnered well with Chopin. He enjoyed simple pleasures such as this.

A self-satisfied smile crossed his face as he remembered when Frederic had played that particular piece for him. It had moved Luca to tears, the emotion, the depth of feeling from the movement as Frederic's long delicate fingers caressed the ivory keys. He had been a genius.

Luca had been the first one to hear it. They had had a few brandies, and Frederic had been excited and bursting with exuberance to play it, and so with a euphoria induced by the alcohol, Frederic played the second piano concerto for Luca. He knew it was a magnificent masterpiece, if only Frederic had lived to see his brilliance appreciated by everyone around the world. Tempus ut semper inimicum.

He took a sip of the whiskey. It was smooth. It was a rich amber colour and a flavour that was sheer nectar on the tongue. Like honey.

Luca glanced at the clock it was almost midnight. As he listened to the music, his thoughts turned to the priest. He was as Demis had said, a devout man, but he was troubled. In Luca's experience, troubled souls almost always strayed from their righteous nature. This man was in danger, but not from anything paranormal, no, the danger here, was mortal in nature. The peril of corruption.

Peo and Bjorn believed that the priest was an exception, they thought he was a good man and could not be corrupted at all. Lanny, on the other hand deemed the priest to be detrimental to them. Lanny was rarely wrong, and he had an incredible gift of reading mortals. He still retained some of his human traits. Something that could be detrimental for an immortal, like a vampire.

But for Luca, he found something in the priest, something that he hadn't seen in a very long time, and he agreed with Peo and Bjorn, this time. The man was intrinsically good, and he put everyone else's wellbeing before his own.

Luca stood up and walked over to the window. He had always been wowed by the metropolis. There was an appeal here, for anyone who was different or who felt unique. LA attracted the weird and the wonderful life forms, that the mortals who inhabited the city couldn't even begin to imagine who they shared their city with. Not all those who shared the city with the humans were bad, some of them, resided and made their living alongside the citizens, they were good, they kept their identities hidden, some could never be recognised as immortal or anything other than human, with similar traits, and personalities like their mortal counterparts.

His phone sprang into life, Luca turned around and glanced over at the armchair where the blue light shone upwards at the ceiling and the vibration from the phone moved it slightly over the arm of the chair. He loved technology. It was so satisfying in its invasion of privacy.

With a deft movement, Luca walked across the room and picked up his phone.

"Hello." He answered casually.

"General, we have some news." It was Peo Satimus.

"What is it?" Luca asked as he picked up the crystal glass and stood up straight.

"We found the lair." Peo said in a quiet tone. "Bjorn is keeping it under surveillance." Luca allowed himself to smile. As always, his officers came through.

"Good but he needs to remain vigilant, the suckers are not unaware of our presence." Luca warned gravely. He too, detested suckers, they were scum who couldn't be trusted.

"Are you coming down to skid row, General?" Peo asked earnestly.

"No, Peo, you can come here," Luca answered. "Bjorn can remain there until dawn." He sipped some whiskey and smiled to himself; he could use some company. "I'll see you shortly." He hung up and put the phone onto the mantlepiece. Luca knew that he probably should go out and investigate with his officers, but he was also aware that the Berserker could handle it.

*****

Luca opened the door of his penthouse apartment and shook hands with Peo and grinned as he let him into the apartment. The Praetorian looked nothing like the multi-millionaire that he was. His dark hair, which was very long, and usually slicked back in a ponytail, now looked dishevelled and the clothes that he now wore, were torn and musty unlike the designer suits that he preferred to wear. Peo looked every inch the vagrant and he smelled like one too. Luca curled his nose in disgust.

"Whiskey?" Luca offered as he led his friend into the lounge.

"Of course." Peo agreed and grinned at him. "Lanny not here?" He looked around but didn't see him.

"No, the Jarl is out." Luca said and handed him the glass. "Looking for romance, no doubt." They both laughed loudly. Lanny was infamous for his romantic exploits. He had been disciplined many times back in the Sixth for his numerous indiscretions.

"He has finally gotten over his broken heart?" Peo joked. "It only took two centuries." Peo laughed heartily.

"You know the Jarl?" Luca said laughing. They all knew that Lanny was a playboy with an inflated ego because of his exceptional good looks.

"He'll be happy to know that he was right, all along." Peo said in a firm tone as he put the glass on the mantlepiece and removed his filthy coat, folded it and put it on the floor, but the smell still lingered.

"How many?" Luca asked as he observed Peo.

"About thirty or so." Peo replied and reached for his glass. "They appear to be organised too." He took another sip of whiskey.

"Organised?" Luca questioned.

"They are here for a reason, General." Peo said seriously. "It's not by chance that they have descended on the city." The whiskey warmed his throat.

"Why do you think they were summoned?" Luca asked him. "By whom? Who would summon suckers into the city?

Don't they know what they do?" This troubled Luca. He had seen it before, when marauding vampires came into town, the devastation that they caused. The mess that they left behind. The Militibus had put a ban on dregs entering the city. It had worked well, until now.

"I don't know who brought them here," Peo spoke in an uneasy tone and looked at Luca with a serious expression on his face. "But I do believe it's connected to the Cyclades." He raised the glass to his mouth. "Those living in the hotel and on skid row are in danger." His voice was as grave as his concern. "They are fodder for these dregs." Luca nodded and agreed with him.

"We have to find the source, discover who is behind this." Luca responded eagerly. "I'll call the Jarl first thing and you get Bjorn, then we'll meet in my office in the morning." Luca said and stood up, he took the glass from Peo and smirked. "Tonight, we shall enjoy some whiskey." They both laughed and Luca refilled the glasses, and they talked about music. He enjoyed Peo's company, they were both Romans and in certain ways enjoyed the simpler things in life, unlike the Vikings, who loved the excesses.

Chapter 11

Bjorn had just put the panigale on its stand when he heard the distinctive purr in the distance. He heard it before he saw it enter the underground car park.

He stood up straight and put his hands on his hips with his legs slightly apart.

The sleek black panigale pulled up next to him and he watched as the rider dismounted. He put the bike on its mount and stood up straight. Bjorn grinned as he observed him. He was always so cocky.

"Peo fixed it up well." Bjorn mused. Neither of them removed their helmets.

"He always does." Lanny said laughing and Bjorn could imagine him smiling underneath the helmet. They walked over to the elevators and pressed the button. "His best paint work yet." They both laughed. Lanny's total disregard for the panigale was a source of amusement for all of them. Except for Peo, it pained him to see what the Jarl did to the bike.

"Do you know why Luca want's us all here so early?" Bjorn asked as they stepped inside the elevator.

"He didn't say." Lanny replied with a cavalier tone, and Bjorn saw him loosen the strap of his helmet.

Whenever they went outside during the day, none of the Militibus removed their helmets. Not because the sun burned them, they weren't photosensitive. UV light did not affect them, once they fed and until it was time for them to return to the Sixth dimension to feed again, which equated to every five months in this dimension. But lately, with the change in the climate, the sun had become stronger, and it affected their mood, too much exposure led to increased irritability and a need to feed sooner. They were aware of how it affected them differently and they dealt with it in their own way, but none of the Militibus allowed themselves to reach the point of dehydration.

The door of the lift opened, and they walked across the lobby to the other elevators which led to Luca's impressive top floor offices.

Neither spoke as the lift stopped and Lanny stepped out first followed by Bjorn and they strode along the corridor to Luca's office. The Vikings were striking in their stature.

Bjorn always smiled at Lanny's insolence about his social position. He never knocked, not even on the General's door. It both amused and irritated them.

Peo and Luca were sitting on the sofa when Bjorn and Lanny entered the office.

"Arrogant as ever, Lanny." Luca jibed with a grin, and the Jarl just laughed.

"Arrogance is something that is perceived, General." Lanny said as he removed his black helmet. "You asked us to come here early, what's the reason for the morning liaison?" He put his helmet onto the arm of the sofa and walked over to the sideboard and poured himself a cup of coffee and then looked at the Militibus.

"Peo and Bjorn have found the lair." Luca confirmed as Lanny rejoined them at the sofa.

"So, there is a lair." He said and took a sip of coffee.

"We followed two suckers, last night." Bjorn said as he put his own helmet on the floor beside the other armchair. "There was about thirty give or take." He had been surprised to find the lair, as usually the street suckers kept their den well hidden. This time, however, it appeared that they wanted to be found.

"They were summoned?" Lanny inquired, incredulously as Peo nodded.

"It seems so." Bjorn replied with a sigh.

"What kind of idiot would bring suckers into the city?" Lanny asked, of no one in particular. "They have to have a reason to trust that scum."

"Scum or not they are here," Peo said as he looked at his comrades. "The homeless are helpless targets at this juncture."

"Do we go after them, while they sleep?" Lanny looked at Luca for affirmation, but he shook his head.

"We have to capture their leader." Luca said firmly. "Find out why they are here and who hired them." Bjorn could see the last thing Lanny wanted was to spare any of them. Bjorn agreed with the Jarl. Suckers were untrustworthy and needed to be removed from the city as quickly as possible too, by whatever means.

"Luca, do you really believe they would give up that information?" Lanny asked in a serious tone. "Even if they knew the real reason they were hired?"

"No, but we have to try." Replied Luca sternly.

"I say we send them to Gehenna." Lanny retorted in an angry tone.

"Patience, Jarl," Peo said trying to dampen the fire in Lanny's temper. "The General is right we can't help the priest without knowing who we are fighting."

"Romani sanguinum!" Lanny retorted and Bjorn saw both Luca and Peo supress a smile. Lanny was a hothead and often acted on impulse, but this time Bjorn agreed with Lanny. They needed to waste them.

"The bloodsuckers are at their weakest right now." Bjorn chimed in and looked at the other Militibus.

"I say if we are to take the leader we move now." Lanny said eagerly. But Luca shook his head again.

"What would that achieve if we go in full of bluster?" Luca asked. "It would only alert them." Bjorn could see that Lanny was getting irritated and so was he. What was the point in waiting? Waiting for what, for more suckers to descend on the city? None of them wanted that.

"You think we should wait?" Bjorn said, but he didn't believe they should.

"Yes, at least until we speak to the priest." Luca responded.

"The priest!" Lanny exclaimed and laughed. "He's soft, he thinks everyone should have redemption." They all looked at him but he just grinned, his anger had dissipated quickly.

"We'll go see him now." Luca said, trying to keep the hostility at bay.

"Sure, let's go see the governor of California as we are at it too." It was clear that Lanny was getting pissed off again.

"General, we should all go see him," Bjorn said. "We can update him on some of the things we have witnessed." Luca agreed and the Militibus left the office and went to call on Father O'Hara at the parochial house.

*****

They were shown into the library by the cheerful old housekeeper. Lanny walked over to the bookcase; he liked the tomes. He was impressed by the extensive range of books the clergyman had but he wasn't going to admit it to any of his comrades. He loved books, and old books in particular.

The door to the library opened and Lanny turned around as a young woman, wearing a black dress and black cardigan came in. Her fair hair was brushed back severely from her face and tied in a bun at the back of her head. She carried a tray with a coffee pot and some pastries.

"Father O'Hara has been called to the phone." She informed them as she put the tray on the coffee table. "Please help yourselves to coffee." She looked at each of them and as she glanced over at Lanny, he saw her lower her eyes as though she couldn't look at him. This amused him.

"Thank you miss." Peo said and smiled at her.

"I'm Sister Angelica." The young woman said, and she glanced at Lanny again. He watched her closely as she retreated out the door. She was pretty but her clothes and hairstyle made her look plain and older than her years. Perhaps that was the idea, not to look attractive at all, but it failed in her case because she was incredibly beautiful.

"Coffee and pastries," Bjorn said smiling. "That sister makes nice treats." Peo and Bjorn laughed as they took a cup and saucer.

"Have some respect," Lanny bawled at them, he was fuming at their lack of reverence. They all looked at him questioningly. He didn't know why, but he was irritated by the jovial banter of his friends, furious by their lack of regard for where they were.

The door opened again and this time, the priest came in. He smiled nervously as he looked at the four Militibus. "Good morning, gentlemen." He said it hesitantly, as no matter what word he used to describe them, felt wrong to him. As he looked at Peo and Bjorn, a look of recognition flashed in his eyes.

"You have met Bjorn and Peo, padre." Lanny said when he saw the recognition in the clergyman's eyes as he came over and took the cup and saucer from the coffee table. "They have been keeping the hotel under surveillance."

"I thought you were familiar." Father O'Hara said. He seemed less relaxed now even though this was the second time that they had met. "Are...are you also-"

"Militibus, yes." Lanny answered for them. He wasn't feeling as friendly as Luca had wanted him to be. He couldn't understand why everything seemed to irritate him at that moment. He wasn't usually this grumpy.

"Vampires, I was going to ask." The priest replied cautiously as the door opened and the nun came in. She had heard what the priest said and glanced at him with a horrified look on her face.

"Vampires, Father?" She asked in dismay as she looked at him with a shocked expression. He nodded. "Surely you don't believe in such a thing." She dismissed, with a wide smile. "You should know better than that." This amused Lanny and he couldn't help grinning at her.

"You're a non-believer?" Lanny asked her but before she could answer him the priest told her they were having a private meeting. The young nun smiled nervously at Lanny and left the library.

"What can I do for you...gentlemen?" Father O'Hara repeated once more.

"The hotel Cyclades, who backed the project?" Luca asked him immediately.

"There were a few backers for it. Let me see." Father O'Hara looked up at the ceiling as he recalled the names of the investors. "There was John Josess, Frank Rostern and an anonymous investor. Why?" Lanny picked up the cup of coffee.

"Were they all willing investors?" Peo asked. The priest looked at him.

"Of course, Frank had an opportunity to develop the hotel into luxury apartments once but when the committee approached him, he had the plans repurposed so the homeless could benefit." Lanny observed the priest closely, either he genuinely believed that there was good in everyone, or the padre was a good actor playing at being naïve, fooling his audience.

"Did they ever say who the other investor was?" Bjorn asked as he watched the older man.

"I did ask, but the other party wished to remain unnamed." Lanny smirked at that, and the priest asked him. "You find something amusing, Mr Lancnut?" Lanny nodded that he did.

"Padre, the hotel sits on a premium site and an anonymous investor remains out of the picture, no recognition for his good deed." Lanny said standing up to his full height of six foot seven. "That doesn't strike you as odd?" He grinned at him. "Well, it does, me."

"No more than you being here in my library." Father O'Hara retorted indignantly. Lanny scowled at him once more as his annoyance returned.

"If you know something, it might help us to discover who is killing the residents and why." Peo stated calmly and stood up and walked over to the window and glanced outside. He was the peacemaker of the group.

"Do you think I would let my parishioners die if I knew who was doing this?" Lanny watched the priest again. Despite his attitude, he could feel the desperation in the old man, he could feel his sadness.

"Padre, when are the remainder of the rooms due to be opened?" Lanny quizzed, softening his tone a little.

"Well, there's a meeting with the committee and the investors, tomorrow afternoon." He was cagy and looked up at Lanny. "Why?"

"Can you invite us, just Luca and me." Lanny said in a critical tone once again.

"I don't believe they would go for strangers coming in on committee business." The fear had returned to his face, but there was something else, something he wasn't letting on.

"Introduce us as investors." Lanny coaxed. "We have certain gifts of observation." He smiled at the priest, trying but failing to put him at ease.

"What Lanny means, Father O'Hara," Luca diplomatically intervened as he stood up also. "We can read situations, that perhaps something will be revealed and." He glanced at Lanny. "Lanny would like to donate financially as well." He grinned at Lanny as Peo and Bjorn snorted. "Wouldn't you Lanny?" Luca pressed but Lanny wasn't impressed at all.

"Of course, General," Lanny said through gritted teeth. They walked over to the door and left.

Chapter 12

Lanny wasn't really convinced that there was anything to be had from the meeting with the priest's committee. It seemed like a waste of time but the General knew best and he was adamant that they exhausted all resources first. Lanny went along with it blindly.

They arrived at the parochial house in Lanny's Porsche SUV. He parked up the car and glanced around the neighbourhood. It wasn't run down but it wasn't prosperous either. But he had no thoughts on it, either way.

"What's on your mind, Jarl?" Luca asked from the seat beside him. Lanny looked across at him and shrugged. They were good friends and could confide in each other about anything. They would die for each other if it came to it. They all would.

"I'm not sure." Lanny admitted and his attention was caught by the nun they had met the previous day. She was tall for a woman and again, like the previous day, she wore a black dress and brogue style shoes. Her hair was pulled back tightly at the back of her head. Even with the plain garb that she wore, she was a beauty. He just couldn't take his eyes off her.

At the distance she was at, Lanny could hear her heart beating and the blood flowing in her veins. He counted the beats, and then he heard several missed beats. He saw that she had noticed him, which accounted for the missed heartbeats.

"We should go inside." Luca interrupted his thought process, and he opened the door. Lanny got out and stood up straight, he shook his head in dismay as he glanced around, the nun was within earshot now. Her smile was wide and infectious as she came close, and Lanny opened the gate for her. He was playing the role of being gallant but there was something else too.

"Good morning, gentlemen." She said in her lyrical voice. "It's such a dull day, isn't it?" Lanny returned her smile. She was having a strange effect on him.

"It's a perfect day." He contradicted, not knowing why and accompanied her up the steps and into the house.

"Father O'Hara is already waiting for you, in his office." Sister Angelica whispered. "I shall bring coffee in shortly." She opened the office door for them. Luca nodded and followed Lanny inside.

Lanny saw the priest sitting behind the old mahogany desk. It dwarfed him. There were three other men sitting around the writing table. They looked from the priest to Lanny and Luca.

"Gentlemen, this is Luca Meridian and Lanny Lancnut." Father O'Hara muttered uneasily as he stood up and the two Militibus vampires came forward and shook hands with the other men. They towered over them.

"We understand from O'Hara," the man with the thick rimmed glasses growled. "That you are keen to donate to the cause." He wore a snide smile and Lanny smelled his corruption, that he wore proudly.

"That's right," Luca said unemotionally. "We have some questions first, though." The office door opened, and Lanny held it open as the young nun came in, struggling with the tray of coffee.

She blushed when Lanny looked at her and took the tray before it fell onto the floor. "Thank you." She said a little flustered. He grinned at her, she was stirring feelings up inside him.

"What questions?" The other man asked. He seemed a little cagey.

"The usual kind." Lanny replied but he was still looking at the nun, she was completely unaware of her effect on him.

"Thank you, Sister Angelica." Father O'Hara snapped and stared at Lanny, as she left the office. "Please, gentlemen sit down." He motioned to the two wooden chairs. Lanny glanced distastefully at them and then back at the priest.

"Thank you, Padre," he nodded slightly as he looked at the priest. "I'll stand." Lanny flashed him a wide smile and it was evident to everyone else that the priest was edgy by their arrival. The atmosphere had changed, the other men were no longer in control of the meeting, the Militibus were now in charge.

"You have questions?" The man asked again, seemingly irritated by the newcomers.

"How many residents do you plan on housing in the building?" Luca asked as he sat back on the wooden chair. Lanny saw him make a face and he smirked at this.

"It can comfortably accommodate one hundred." The other man said and gave a cough. Lanny looked at him, his eyes bore into his mind. He heard the blood course through his veins and smelt the pheromones he gave off, it was putrid. Vile.

"Only one hundred?" Luca queried and then exchanged a look with Lanny.

"For safety reasons," John Josess added quickly but looked very nervous at the sight of the Militibus.

"The building has twelve floors." Luca insisted. The other man laughed but it sounded more like a grunt as he picked up the cup and saucer and took a sip and Lanny observed him carefully. Of the three committee members, he was giving off the most offensive pheromones.

"Young man...I've forgotten your name." He said as he addressed Luca condescendingly.

"Luca Meridian."

"Mr Meridian, the building is in a prime location but unfortunately the residents are far from ideal." He replaced the cup and saucer on the desk. Lanny despised him immediately.

"Meaning?" Lanny pressed him hard and stared in his direction.

"Meaning only that they are drug addicts and drunks, not exactly model tenants." He said harshly. "Suicide is high amongst them, be it overdose or thinking they can fly." He grunted a laugh again as he looked at Lanny. "Perhaps you could use your daddy's money investing in horses or something more your style, young man." Lanny stood up straight and grinned at him. He was an egotistical individual. He was comfortable in his greed, and he didn't care who knew it.

"Perhaps," Lanny countered. "But where is the satisfaction in that." He flashed him a brilliant smile.

"You mentioned suicide," Luca said as he deliberately brought the conversation back to the building in question.

"There have been a few." John Josess confirmed. But as he looked at the other man, he seemed to regret it as the look which passed between them suggested he was too open. Lanny quickly picked up on it and glanced knowingly at Luca.

"I have heard there were twelve." Lanny responded and looked him straight in the eyes. The man shifted uneasily in his chair under the weight of Lanny's stare.

"They weren't able to be rehabilitated." The other man said quickly.

"Really?" Lanny said smirking and he looked at the priest with a smile on his face. "Surely everyone can be redeemed with the right intervention." He saw the sides of the padre's mouth twitch as he suppressed a laugh.

"Some are, but most are not worth saving." Josess said uncomfortably. "Why should you care?" Lanny stared at him again and sneered. He liked none of the three men in the room, he certainly didn't trust them.

"When I invest several million dollars," Lanny quipped as he took out his cheque book. "I want to make sure my investment is worth my time." The two men stared at each other. Their interests were piqued.

Lanny observed that since the meeting began, the third man sitting at the far end of the desk had remained silent. Lanny looked at him, his heart was beating normally, he appeared unstressed, unmoved.

"Well, we thank you Mr..."

"Lancnut." Lanny said and walked over to the desk and picked up the silver pen, he looked at the priest and quickly wrote the cheque, tore it from the book, folded it and handed it to Father O'Hara. The transaction was quick.

The three men stood up and so did the priest and they shook hands with the Militibus as they left the room. Lanny and Luca hung back and waited for the priest to return. Neither of them said anything.

"Well, what did you learn from the meeting?" Father O'Hara asked as he came back into the office, he still held the cheque in his hand as he glanced awkwardly at the vampires.

"That they are a greedy bunch, you have done business with Padre." Lanny replied, without any filter to his mouth, and watched as the priest held out his hand to give him back the cheque. "Keep it, invest it as you see fit in the hotel." Lanny said and the priest looked astonished. This made him smile, it was clear that the clergyman was unused to donations of this kind.

"Who was the silent one?" Luca asked as he stood up, he shook his legs, he was stiff from sitting on the uncomfortable chair.

"That was Bishop Corkery's secretary." Father O'Hara answered and went over to the door. "Sister Angelica, can you come here." He called out and a few moments later the door opened, and the young nun came in.

"Yes, Father?" Lanny looked at her, she fascinated him, and he would like to get to know her in every way possible.

"Can you bring fresh coffee, please."

"Not for us." Luca said and looked at Lanny. "I have a meeting with Demis." He smiled and to his disappointment, Lanny walked with him. He shook hands with the priest and then gently took the young nun's hand in his. Her skin was soft, but it felt cold. She shivered at his touch.

"You need to get that coldness seen to." Lanny said to her in a gentle tone.

"Coldness?" She replied curiously. "I have always had cold hands." Lanny looked fixedly at her. "It's a sign of a warm heart." She smiled at him and then looked quickly away. He felt like he wanted to stay and talk to her.

"Lanny," Luca called out to him, he sounded irritated, and he looked over at him and joined him in the hallway.

They walked out into the grey afternoon and over to Lanny's SUV and drove back to Luca's office.

Lanny's mind was elsewhere, back at the parochial house with the beautiful young nun.

Chapter 13

Lanny dropped Luca off and drove away. He needed to think. He drove out along the Pacific coast highway. He turned on the stereo as he drove and the familiar piano playing of Clara's concerto caressed his ears. But his mind was preoccupied, somewhere else.

As Lanny drove along the coast his thoughts turned to the one mortal woman who had taken his heart and played with him. Clara had shown him how to pursue and to fall madly in love, but the cruelty in her teasing of him was as legendary as her music and piano playing.

A smile crossed his face as he remembered the big seduction, that he had made toward her and afterward, how her rebuff of him was a little too feigned, because some weeks later she had seduced him again, this time in the garden of her home in Vienna.

He pulled over and lay back into the seat. His thoughts turned to the nun. She had piqued his interest in a way no woman had before. Of course, Lanny knew that as a servant of the church, the nun would never give herself to him, but he couldn't help feeling attracted to her. Lanny didn't know what it was about her, but she awakened a feeling inside of him and he had never felt like that before, at least not since he became a Militibus. Not even with Clara.

It was difficult for Lanny to call himself a vampire. He was unlike the bloodsuckers that walked the streets at night in search of a victim to bleed. Lanny didn't hunt for victims, as his feeding was taken care of by the gourmet production line that produced the blood for their feeding every five months. Their blood lust was controlled, and they didn't just feed on any kind of blood from just anyone. The council of Elders took their supply from carefully selected aristocrats who were pampered and taken care of, so the Militibus didn't resort to the blood addicted habits of the street suckers. No, the Militibus were the elite and behaved as such, and in a manner which was expected of them.

Lanny laid his head back against the head rest and closed his eyes briefly and an image of Sister Angelica flashed before them. Her beautiful smile, her beautiful body hidden by the plain clothing she wore. Her beauty sublimed because of the institution she belonged to. He was enchanted by this mortal female, not as he had been with Clara. He felt the hardening in his pants as he thought of her.

Lanny glanced in the rear-view mirror and saw a motorbike pull in and then a car. He looked in the glass as the rider dismounted the bike and walked with a swagger back to the car. Immediately, Lanny knew that it was a dreg. His demeanour gave him away. He observed the scene from his car.

He looked closer to see if he could make out the driver but all he could see was a hand. The driver of the car handed the sucker a canister and a brown bag. The transaction was suspicious in the early evening, it looked as though it were some kind of rendezvous, that certainly had a sinister appearance to it.

Lanny turned around and saw the sucker walk back to the bike and kick start it once more. The bike passed him at speed, but Lanny wasn't interested in the dreg, he was interested in the car and its driver. Who was it? Was the driver a mortal or monster? If he was mortal, did he know that his companion was a street sucker? Did he even care?

The car passed him, and Lanny waited for a few moments before starting the SUV and he followed at a discreet distance. He didn't know if it was significant or not to what they were investigating, but he had to check it out, one way or another. A dreg involved a crime of some sort, that much was clear.

The traffic began to build as they approached the city once more. Lanny didn't detect whether the driver was aware if he were being followed or not. Either way, Lanny didn't care he was just focussed on the task at hand. He needed to know what was going on.

He had to swerve violently as a truck crossed lanes in front of him. As he braked hard and recovered the SUV, he looked for the car he had been tailing but it had gone. He wondered if the driver had turned off for Santa Monica.

"Maledicere!" Lanny swore in Latin as he drove on. He had lost the car and the driver. He sighed audibly and hit the steering wheel.

There was no point in trying to second guess what turn the car and its occupant had taken, they were gone, Lanny had lost them thanks to the idiot truck. He was sure that he could have successfully trailed them but now he would never know. He decided he would go home and change and go out to the Berserker's club and enjoy an evening's entertainment, perhaps pick up a female too.

Chapter 14

Bjorn was sitting in his office when he noticed Lanny was at the bar. He was alone. He didn't know that the Militibus were coming to the club that night. Bjorn stood up and closed the button of his tailored suit. He walked over to the door, opened it and walked down the tempered glass steps and into the nightclub.

As he made his way over to the bar, he was greeted by a man he had done business with a few times before. He had purchased some rare vinyl records from the nineteen sixties from him. "How are you, Mr Azelason?" The man greeted Bjorn with a friendly smile. "I got in a special consignment." Bjorn looked at him and tried to leave. "A custom-built guitar. I think you should take a look, I'm sure you'll be impressed."

"Maybe later, enjoy your evening and have a bottle of champagne on the house." Bjorn snapped his fingers at a passing waiter and told him to bring a bottle of champagne to the party in the centre booth. He strode purposefully across to the bar.

Bjorn slapped Lanny on the back and sat down on the stool next to him. "Hey there." Bjorn said and raised a finger to the barman to bring two drinks.

"Good evening." Lanny said and grinned at him. "How's business?" The nightclub was full and as Lanny had made his way into the club there had been a line waiting to get in.

"Good, are the Romans joining you?" Bjorn asked as the barman put the whiskey on the counter in front of them.

"I don't know." Lanny said a little vaguely.

"What's wrong, Jarl?" He asked as he reached for the glass.

"I lost a lead I was tailing earlier." Lanny replied and took a sip of his drink. "Iubentium." Bjorn raised his glass.

"Was it connected to the case?" Lanny shook his head.

"I don't know, Bjorn, but a damn truck cut across my path, and I lost the car." Lanny said and grinned at his friend. "So, I ended up here." He motioned cheers and took a gulp of the exceptional beverage, and they both laughed.

"Good choice of establishment." Bjorn agreed grinning at him.

He looked out over to the dance floor and smiled when he saw the revellers dancing. The music choice wasn't exactly his taste, but Bjorn knew that the deejay he employed at the club was one of the best in Southern California.

"Are you and Peo checking out skid row tonight?" Lanny asked casually and looked back at the dancefloor.

"No, not tonight." Bjorn responded, he had other plans for the night, and Lanny quickly picked up on the twinkle in his eyes.

"You're entertaining?" But Bjorn just laughed.

"Jarl, that's none of your business." Bjorn said and slapped him jovially on the back.

"I'll take a walk down skid row, check it out." Lanny reacted. This surprised Bjorn because Lanny didn't like to go to skid row, at least not if he could help it.

"You're sure?" He quipped, surprised by the statement, as he grinned at his friend. He didn't understand the sudden change in the Jarl.

"I sometimes do surveillance, Berserker." He replied good humouredly. They both laughed and Bjorn watched as he downed the whiskey in one gulp, and they slapped each other on the arm and Lanny left the club.

*****

Lanny walked confidently down the sidewalk, there were the usual group of people sitting down on the ground, settling in for the night ahead. Some were arguing with themselves over something important in their own minds. They were some huddled over an oil barrel warming their hands and they spoke in hushed tones as Lanny passed them. He could hear the erratic beats from their hearts and the rush of their blood.

He saw the lights on in the Cyclades on several floors. It looked quiet. Normal, almost. Lanny walked purposefully over to the glass door and glanced casually inside. The concierge was standing behind the desk, he was reading a newspaper, oblivious to the goings on outside. The lobby was empty. He sniffed the air, there were no suckers around.

Lanny walked on a little further and he saw the lights on in the soup kitchen which was run by Father O'Hara. There was no one inside but then he noticed the nun. She was wiping down a food cupboard. He stopped for a moment, just to observe her from where he stood. She was happy, he could sense from her manner, from her movements. Then with his astute hearing, he heard the slight hum as she sang a song, sweet and lyrical, but he couldn't understand the words.

He walked over to the door and tried the handle, it turned, and the door opened. Lanny went inside. The nun came out of the kitchen and was about to say something when she saw it was Lanny. "Oh, hello, Mr Lancnut."

"Hello Sister Angelica." He said and smiled warmly at her as he looked longingly at her. She glanced up at him quietly.

"It's late, what has you out and about?" She asked a little shyly and she walked over to the door and locked it. Lanny looked at her and smiled amiably at her again. He knew that it was wrong to be looking at her the way that he was, but at that moment, Lanny didn't care. He was attracted to her, and he couldn't help the way he felt.

"Please call me Lanny," he said and stood up straight. "I came out for a walk and ended up here." He grinned as he saw her expression change. It was clear that she didn't believe him.

"Nobody ends up willingly on skid row." Sister Angelica said readily. Her whole face lit up when she smiled, and she was completely unaware of her alure, but he was more than aware, he felt it in the tightening of his pants.

"Would you believe me if I told you I wanted to make sure those people out there were alright?" He asked seriously as he watched her walk back over to the kitchen, he followed her.

"There aren't many rich people who care about those poor souls out there." She said in a helpless tone. "To most people, they shouldn't even be seen." Sister Angelica sounded as desperate as the priest.

"The padre has done his best to house them." Lanny responded as he looked at the young woman.

"Father O'Hara has a heart of gold." She said beaming up at him. "He believes everyone should have a second chance." This made Lanny smirk as he remembered the brief conversation he had had with the priest. He would enjoy another discussion with him.

"What about you, Sister?" Lanny asked in a serious tone. "What do you believe?" She walked over to him and looked up into his face, he noticed her blush as she watched him and then shyly, she lowered her eyes.

"Everyone deserves to have a second chance." Sister Angelica said almost in a whisper. "Some people just need a little help to find their way again." Lanny glanced into her eyes; they were a beautiful shade of green. They were filled with life, a life filled with hope. Just for a moment he wondered what it would be like to wake up and have those eyes look at him.

"How long have you worked here?" Lanny asked her. She giggled shyly.

"Almost four years in this parish." Sister Angelica responded. "I came out here after I graduated." He looked at her questioningly. "When I became a junior sister." She replied to his questioning look. He grinned, not taking his eyes off her, she unwittingly commanded him to look at her.

"Do you like being a nun?" Lanny asked interested as he stood up to his full height and towered over her.

"It was my calling." Sister Angelica told him, and he saw her smile fade just slightly as she looked at him. "I wanted to serve God and do good wherever He sent me."

"Would you like to have a coffee with me?" He asked her suddenly. The nun seemed to freeze with shock for a moment. "It's only coffee, Sister." Lanny reassured her when he saw the look on her face. He needed to spend some time alone with her, he couldn't let her go that quickly.

"OK, Mr Lancnut."

"Lanny." He corrected her gently with a broad smile on his face.

He opened the door for her, and he followed her outside and waited as she locked the door. Lanny walked beside her, and next to him she seemed tiny, dainty. He could smell the soap that she washed with, and it mixed with the smell of cooking, but it was her hormones which excited him and had his feelings in a whirl.

They walked on a small distance away from skid row and then turned onto Main and walked a little further.

There was an all-night café and Lanny opened the door as the nun walked in first. They sat at the booth near the window and ordered coffee. Lanny watched her as she glanced around the café. He knew that she was feeling a little awkward being in a public place with a man. This amused him. Everything about this sensual woman interested him.

"Tell me more about the project to house the residents." Lanny asked her as the server brought them their coffee. He noticed the nun glance gauchely at the girl and then she lowered her eyes. She seemed socially awkward, or maybe it was just around him.

"Father O'Hara didn't have an easy time convincing the committee or the investors that it was worth doing." Sister Angelica said in a low tone after the server had gone. "There were quite a few against the idea." Lanny gazed at her. She looked flushed, almost like she was betraying someone.

"Who were against it?" He pressed her for an answer, but he was also careful in his questioning so as not to frighten her and then she probably would end up not saying anything at all.

"Frank Rostern for one." She answered and he could sense she was getting angry at the mention of his name. He jumped on this quickly.

"But isn't he a major backer for the project?" Lanny quizzed. She nodded. "What changed his mind?" Sister Anjelica leaned forward and so did Lanny, then she said in a low tone.

"Only because of the publicity involved with it." Sister Angelica leaned back again, and she reached for the coffee cup. He watched her carefully, but she was painfully shy, and it showed.

"Publicity?" Lanny challenged and looked at her intently.

"Yes, he's only doing it because he sees it as a way into politics, they both do." She said in an aroused voice now. "They don't care about those people as long as it looks good for them." The nun was becoming emotional now.

"So, if it were to fail, this Rostern and Josess wouldn't succeed either?" He saw her smile, it was a beautiful smile, just like her.

"Mr Lancnut...Lanny," She corrected herself with a giggle and he beamed at her too. "Either way, they win. Rostern holds the planning for its use, be it for the homeless housing scheme or if it failed, it can be developed into luxury condominiums, my guess is he hopes it fails." Lanny stared at her for a moment. It figured. There was no way that they could lose out. The parish or the city would pay regardless.

"The priest knows this?" He asked her seriously.

"Of course, but..." She looked around her. "I don't think Rostern can repurpose it, he probably needs the consent of the owner, and the city." This was important information which had been withheld from them, either knowingly or unwittingly by the priest.

"Who's the owner?"

"No one knows for certain." She replied. "There's lots of speculation on that front." This was the vital information that Lanny needed but didn't have. The project was being jeopardised deliberately it would seem. *But by whom?*

"Sister Angelica, can you do me a favour?" He asked her gently. She nodded. "Can you have the padre meet with me and Luca tomorrow?" She stared at him with wide eyes. "It's important." He reassured and smiled at her once more. "Now, I shall take you home." He left some money on the table, and they left the café and went out into the night.

Chapter 15

Luca was sitting with his leg lazily over the other in the large penthouse. As he glanced around it, he was impressed. Lanny had incredibly taste when it came to fine art. Some of the pieces on the wall were, he knew, from raids that the Jarl had made with the famous Viking, Birgerarne. The fine tapestry which hung above the extensively stocked drinks cabinet was from Lindisfarne. It depicted a scene from the library with the monks in the scriptorium. They all knew that it was Lanny's favourite. Not least because it served as a reminder of the raid he had done, and what had happened during it.

"General, I had a conversation with the nun last night." Lanny called out as he came into the lounge.

"Oh?" Luca said with a smile. He suspected that his second in command had more than just a working interest in the woman. "What was the conversation about, or is it something you can share?" He asked with a knowing grin, but Lanny's expression was a serious one.

"The hotel is owned privately," he divulged. "The owner, it would appear, and no one seems to know who he is, is set to make a fortune if the building is turned into luxury condominiums." Luca stared at him. He hadn't suspected something like this.

"How does the nun know this?" Luca asked as he wiped some dust from his leg. "Can we trust what she is saying?" He looked up at Lanny.

"Why would she lie, Luca?" Lanny asked curiously as he sat down on the armchair across from him. It wasn't like the Jarl to be so protective, Luca thought to himself.

"Why indeed?" Luca responded eventually. There were lots of theories, lots of reasons why the housing of the homeless in the hotel shouldn't go ahead. It's reputation for one, would have any superstitious mortal running in the opposite direction. Yet, here, Father O'Hara had pulled off a coup de gras, first in acquiring the hotel, then turning it into sheltered accommodation for his parishioners. Yet why was someone determined to jeopardise the entire operation, other than to rid the area of the homeless but that too, had its problem.

"Luca, I think the planning officer, Rostern and the builder, Josess are the ones who have brought the suckers into the city." Lanny said abruptly, as he sat back in the chair. "They reek of corruption."

"But for what purpose? To scare the homeless out of the hotel?" Luca questioned more of himself than of Lanny. "Even if they were to develop the hotel into luxury condos, they still have the issue of the tents pitched outside."

"That is what makes no sense at all." Lanny pondered. "I've asked Sister Angelica to tell the padre we want to meet with him later." Luca stared at him and nodded. There was a softness to the Jarl's voice as he said the nun's name. But Luca decided not to tease him about it. It might just be a sensitive subject for Lanny, he thought.

"Let us go and see what the padre knows." Luca said rising from the armchair.

*****

They drove in silence to the priest's house. Both Militibus were lost in their own thoughts and reveries.

Lanny parked outside the parochial house and switched off the engine. He looked around at the other buildings. They were in reasonable condition, but at a closer look they showed the lack of investment by the owners of the properties, this brought the neighbourhood down, somewhat.

They got out of the car and walked purposefully up the now familiar concrete steps and rang the doorbell.

A short while later, Sister Angelica opened the door and she smiled widely at Lanny, he tenderly returned her smile. "Is the padre here?" He asked in his baritone voice, and she blushed.

"Waiting for you both in the library." Sister Angelica said almost flirtatiously to him, and she led them into the hallway.

Lanny knocked on the door and without waiting for a reply he opened the door and strode into the library.

"Ah Mr Lancnut and Mr Meridian, I've been expecting you." Father O'Hara said as he stood up and held out his hand to both. "Sister Angelica was insistent you needed to talk with me."

"You're troubled, padre." Lanny commented as he studied the expression on the older man's face. He couldn't hide it.

"This is a troubling time." Father O'Hara reposted curtly and almost as soon as he had said it, he seemed to regret it. "Please, sit down." He motioned to them to sit by the fire.

"I sense something else is troubling you." Lanny insisted. "Not just the hotel."

"You are perceptive, Mr Lancnut." Father O'Hara ventured, and his head hung in a worried way. "I had news this morning that Grace, one of my resident's threw herself from the roof area this morning just before dawn." Luca and Lanny just looked at each other. "I don't understand what she was doing up there, she's afraid of heights, you see." He blessed himself. Lanny sensed that he did that a lot.

"I thought the levels beyond the seventh floor was unavailable to the residents." Luca uttered as he studied the priest carefully.

"That's right the lift doesn't go up beyond there yet." Father O'Hara said. "The only way up is on the fire escape and Grace wouldn't do that." He was beside himself with grief.

"You're sure?" Luca quizzed him. The priest nodded.

"I was there last night," Lanny interposed harshly. "Just after midnight, I didn't sense dregs nearby." He looked at Luca, who nodded. "I saw nothing out of the ordinary, General."

"Who is doing this to my flock?" The priest asked in a despairing voice. "These people have nothing, but they are being hunted and slaughtered. Why?"

"Sister Angelica, told me that the building is privately owned." Lanny persisted and looked up as the door opened and the young nun came in with a tray. Lanny smiled warmly at her as she placed the tray on the coffee table, and she glanced shyly back at him.

"Thank you, Sister." Father O'Hara said, and the nun left the room. "She has a good heart, the homeless people at the soup kitchen are very fond of her." The priest said and then sighed.

"Padre, do you know who owns that building?" Lanny asked outright.

"No, I told you already, it was an anonymous donor." He replied. "A generous offer made for the benefit of the area." Lanny wasn't so sure but said nothing.

"Indeed, but perhaps not for the use it has right now." Luca said playing devil's advocate as he looked him straight in the eye.

"What are you suggesting, Mr Meridian?" Father O'Hara snapped and then. "Forgive me, this business is upsetting." He added directly. "My temper is frayed."

"What we are suggesting, Father O'Hara," Luca said. "Is whoever owns that building does not want it to house homeless drug addicts but wants to develop it into something else." The older man stared at him dubiously.

"That's preposterous, young man." He refuted vehemently.

"Is it, padre?" Lanny questioned. "What exactly do you know about Rostern and Josess?" Father O'Hara smirked at him disbelievingly and shook his head.

"You really can't be serious?" His voice questioned their suggestion as if it were a personal insult directed at him.

"What do you know?" Lanny pressed him hard for an answer.

"They are respected citizens and have given their time free of charge to this project." The priest was aroused now, and Lanny could hear his heart pounding in his chest. He could hear the struggle of the beats and he knew that the older man was labouring with his dilemma. His heart was labouring to pump the blood through his veins.

"Father O'Hara, you are a good man," Luca said trying to defuse the tension, by softening his tone. "But it is our experience that some people see potential in their exploitation of those lesser off in society." Father O'Hara glared at him.

"A vampire is telling me that the generosity of two selfless individuals is questionable?" He looked from one to the other and sneered. "You expect me to accept the word of two murderers?" Both Militibus glared at him angrily. He was out of order.

"Now hold on a second, padre," Lanny said in a raised voice and getting to his feet. "We are Tempus Militibus officers, not murderers as you call us. We are here to help you. We get nothing out of this."

"Lanny, stand down." Luca ordered. "Father O'Hara doesn't mean it like that, do you Father?"

"Of course, you get something out of it," the priest argued with him. "By the very insult, you gave to Rostern and Josess. You assume everyone is out for themselves as both of you are."

"Evidently, padre," Lanny quarrelled as he glared at the priest. "What you have learnt in your book went completely over your head. Good day." Lanny strode over to the door and walked out into the hall and left the building.

He sat into the SUV and waited for Luca. He was angry. Angrier than he had been in a very long time. How dare the clergyman question him or his bona fides. He had honour, he was not a killer as he had implied.

Chapter 16

The pale blue paintwork on the wing of the Buick, slowly but surely began to blend in with the remainder of the paint on the classic car. The light blue and grey leather seats, which had been torn and ripped now, showed no sign of having ever had any wear and tear to them. The chrome on the dashboard and the steering wheel gleamed. It was a work of art once more.

Peo stood back and smiled wryly as he admired the restoration work, he had done on the car. He was proud of it. Although it wasn't close to being finished, there was just a few things left, like trying to source the wheels and white walled tyres. He was working on that, there had been a few leads, but they weren't from the year that the car was originally manufactured. Only original parts were used in all the restorations that Peo did. It was why his reputation was second to none. It was his meticulous attention to detail and use of only genuine parts that had his work so respected amongst enthusiasts.

He nodded and appreciated the design and engineering that had gone into this beautiful piece of car history.

Peo walked over to the bench where the various polishes and cloths were stored, he picked up the red microfibre cloth and walked back over to the car and began to wipe the headlight. This car would be a beauty once more, he thought to himself as he polished the light with the soft cloth. *Perfection!*

"You are very thorough with all your restorations." Peo stood up and smiled at his friend. "When will it be finished?"

"As soon as I can get the wheels and tyres." Peo said and grinned. "What brings you to the garage, Luca?" Peo walked over to the roller door and pressed the button, and it began to roll down and he walked back over to the car and beamed when he saw the impressed look on the General's face. They were always in awe of his work.

"Needed a break from the office." Luca replied with a huge grin on his face.

"Wouldn't Bjorn's club provide a better distraction?" Peo teased. "A drink?" Luca nodded and they retreated upstairs to Peo's home.

He walked over to the drinks cabinet and poured two generous glasses of whiskey. Peo handed one to Luca. "Vestram salutem." He said as he raised the glass.

"I am impressed with the whiskey, Peo." Luca said after he took a sip. "New consignment?" The two romans laughed. Whiskey was their tipple of choice.

"You're not the only one to appreciate good whiskey, Luca." Peo said and laughed. "The Jarl would be impressed too, don't you think?" They both chuckled raucously.

"Do you think anything impresses Lanny?" Luca said as he took another sip.

"Lanny impresses Lanny." Peo said and grinned. "You seem concerned over something, General, what is it?" He had served with Luca for a long time, and he knew when the Centurian was worried, and this was one of those times.

"Lanny discovered something the other night, from the nun." Luca said and sat back on the plush sofa. "It would appear the building is owned by an unknown benefactor." Peo nodded. He wasn't surprised by this revelation.

"That's not really surprising, a lot of these places are owned privately." Peo said easily. He had learned that the twenty first century held no surprises and when one accepted that, life was simple as were people's actions. He was being rather philosophical now.

"True but the priest seems to believe that there is nothing suspicious about recent events in connection to two of the benefactors." Luca said and mused at the building situation.

"Who are they and what are their roles?" Peo asked shortly. He had done some business deals that were questionable and with individuals that were unsavoury, but he didn't care as long as the deal was done. It certainly didn't mean he was corrupt, far from it.

"One is the planner, and the other is the builder." Luca replied and looked carefully at Peo, to gage his reaction. "Lanny and the priest had a heated encounter." Peo grinned at this, and it wasn't a surprise to him either that Lanny would have a hostile confrontation with the priest, sooner or later. His feelings toward him were not hidden. The Jarl was very transparent.

"Lanny cares little about other's opinion if it runs contrary to his own." Peo reasoned.

"Only in this case," Luca rallied and emptied the contents of the glass in a single gulp. "The Jarl has grounds for his suspicion." Luca defended Lanny.

"Really?" Luca nodded and Peo tightened his jaw, the Jarl had an uncanny sense for suspicious activities.

"Lanny is always meticulous in his investigation and the other day when we met with the investors, they seemed uncomfortable with us."

"Did they suspect what you are?" Peo enquired and went over to the dresser and picked up the bottle of whiskey and brought it back over to the where they were sitting.

"No, I don't think they did." Luca replied candidly. "But if what Lanny believes is true," Luca paused as he took the glass from Peo. "Then someone in that committee has hired suckers to rid the hotel of its residents." They both looked at each other. The mood had just changed.

"Where's Lanny now?" Peo asked, looking at the General.

"I think he has gone to seek solace somewhere." He grinned and downed the whiskey. "Peo, you and I are going to the lair, get Bjorn and meet me in an hour at the hotel." Luca stood up and Peo walked with him to the door.

"What about the Jarl?" Peo tested. If they were going to check out the lair, he preferred to have Lanny with them. He may be a hot head, but he was lethal with the sword and the axe.

"I'll call over to his apartment now." Luca offered and slapped him on the arm and left.

Peo closed the door behind him and walked down the hallway and into his bedroom. He changed into the clothes he wore when he patrolled: Leather trousers, leather jacket, boots and black tee shirt. His signature uniform.

Chapter 17

The Militibus rode in perfect synchronicity on their sleek panigales. Each of them dressed and ready for action. Excited for the chase as always.

The powerful purr of the engines was like a perfectly executed symphony as they put the bikes on their stands. One by one the four vampires dismounted from their bikes and stood up straight. They synchronously glanced around in different directions.

Luca removed his helmet first and checked the inside pocket of his long leather coat, his dagger was readily accessible. Then he felt the cold handle of his roman sword as he flicked the button on his scabbard. Luca looked at the tall handsome Jarl as he removed his helmet and his sleek blond hair fell like a golden mane down his back. Lanny removed his axe and his sword from their holders inside his leather coat. Bjorn was already striding toward the alleyway followed by Peo. They were all ready and poised for the encounter that was about to occur. The atmosphere was palpable.

Before they entered the alley, Luca said in a low tone to his comrades. "We know why we are here, to take the leader." They all nodded except for Lanny. "Jarl Lancnut, we take him alive, OK?" Lanny looked at the General and flashed him a brilliant smile, as his handsome face lit up at the thoughts of a fight.

"Of course, General." But Luca wasn't convinced by his tone. Luca shook his head, there was no controlling Lanny when a raid was imminent.

"OK let's go but be on your guard." They nodded and quietly made their way down the alley to the entrance of the building, that led down to the sewers.

Carefully, the Militibus prised the door open and one by one filed into the narrow walkway and noiselessly descended the steps into the sewer. As they descended the odour assaulted their nostrils.

Making their way along the passageway, each of them watched and observed closely as they walked stealthily along the pitch-black tunnel. Their vampiric vision as clear as daylight.

They stopped and looked around, then nodded at each other as they split off in pairs moving in opposite directions. Their goal was to take out silently, as many of the lair as they could and then capture the leader. It wasn't going to be an easy task, given how many dregs were likely in the lair. But there were four of them, each an elite swordsman.

Lanny and Peo made their way along the darkened passageway, the stench of decay along with the smell of suckers was overpowering, oppressive even. It reeked of death, from mortal to rodent. The nest didn't care which victim they killed, as long as they satiated their blood addiction.

Lanny and Peo were experienced soldiers and had fought many battles together and each covered the other's back when needed. The Viking Jarl depended on the Roman Praetorian and vice versa.

Lanny stopped suddenly and nodded to Peo and indicated over to where two bloodsuckers were lying on the ground, unconscious, their coats filthy with traces of dried blood on the lapels. Peo gestured to where he spotted two more, huddled over in armchairs. Lanny signalled to move in for a quick kill. It was clear that the dregs in the armchair were drunk and had passed out from the effects of drinking the blood of a seriously inebriated victim or victims. Lanny grinned as he glanced at Peo. This was what they both enjoyed, the finishing off, of the parasites they were hunting.

Noiselessly each of the Militibus made their way over to the suckers, with their weapons raised, they came down hard on the vampires' heads and decapitated them in one fell swoop. With lightning speed they threw the severed heads onto the bodies and stepped away quickly from the remains as a bright light enveloped the slain chumps and reduced them to a pile of soot, sending them successfully to the Tenth.

Lanny and Peo made their way deeper into the lair and with each step that they took it brought them closer to the foulest stench, which meant a pile of decaying bodies. They were on heightened alert also as the hoods they hunted could rouse at any given moment. They knew that the lair was a large one and that the suckers, even in their sleepy state could be dangerous.

A slight movement caught Peo's attention and Lanny quickly looked over to the source. A large rat scurried across the path where an undead deviant was beginning to stir. They both remained very still for a moment.

Quickly Lanny did a scan of the vicinity and nodded to Peo to take out the sucker. As the Praetorian beheaded the vampire, Lanny continued into the darkened walkway.

Walking carefully and close to the wall, as close as he could, Lanny stepped on a tin can, and it scurried along the ground loudly in front of him. He closed his eyes, furious with himself. How could he have been so stupid not to have seen it?

"Gehenna!" He gabbled as Peo caught his arm and hurried ahead of the Jarl.

Lanny was more alert now as he followed the Praetorian, and they entered the lair. He knew that the leeches surely had heard it. Then suddenly, a light lit up the subterranean room and a sucker stood in front of the Militibus, their formation about ten deep. He was laughing as he came forward and looked with disdain at the Militibus standing in the cavern. Lanny cursed himself for being so careless.

"Well, well, look who we have here." The scrounger said and laughed sarcastically. "Gentlemen, you should have told us you were visiting." The other suckers jeered loudly, and Lanny and Peo looked at each other, they were pissed off now. "We'd have made a cake."

"This isn't a social call, dreg." Lanny said, unable to disguise his disgust at having to breathe the same air as these scum.

"Just as well, I didn't have time to clean up." Some of the undead leeches high fived and laughed but the leader raised his hand to silence them. He had just outed himself.

"We don't want any trouble." Peo said diplomatically and looked at the dreg.

"You don't want trouble?" The leader said and stepped forward. Peo stood up straight, his hand tight on the sword. "That's why you wasted my friends, my family?" The street vampire came closer. There was a loud uproar from the men behind him. "Silence." He roared and looked over his shoulder, without warning Lanny deftly grabbed him and with his axe at the leader's throat he roared.

"Tell me what I want to know, and you won't go to Gehenna." The sucker laughed loudly but Lanny scraped the sharp axe against his neck. He was in no mood to play the vampire's game.

"I have nothing to say to you." The killer said and spat on the ground. "The Militibus can suck me off."

"That is unfortunate then." Lanny said and looked at Peo, who shook his head with a warning. They were to take the leader alive. "Very unfortunate for you."

"Call off your bandits." Peo said angrily and held out his hand in front of him as he looked at the others cagily making their way over to them, he knew it could go bad at any minute.

"If I don't?" The leader asked sneering at Peo, showing his blood-stained teeth.

"If you don't," Lanny growled and pressed the blade of his sword against the vampire's ribs. "I will send you to Gehenna, sucker." The street slayer laughed loudly and struggled against Lanny, but he wasn't as strong as the Militibus officer. "Just give me a reason to." The Jarl jeered at him.

"I don't fear you, there's eleven of us and only two of you." The killer heckled as he tried to struggle free of the Jarl's grip.

"You sure about that?" Peo jibed as he raised his sword in a quick movement and beheaded two suckers. Without warning the skirmish began resulting in the street thugs being wiped out as Luca and Bjorn joined Peo in obliterating them. The suckers didn't know what hit them.

The leader struggled against Lanny, but his grip was vice like.

The Militibus came forward to the hoodlum and Luca smiled at him and said in a firm tone. "We want to know who invited you here?" The sucker laughed and spat at Luca.

"Watch your manners, scumbag." Bjorn bellowed at him and connected with a left hook to his jaw.

"Who hired you?" Luca interrogated. Again, the sucker just laughed and struggled with Lanny, but the Jarl was more formidable than the other vampire.

"General," Lanny said, and Luca looked at him. "This skinner is not the leader." Peo nodded in agreement with the Jarl.

"Yes I am." The sucker protested vehemently as Lanny let him go and pushed him into the centre of the cavern where the Militibus surrounded him.

"Let me finish him, General." Lanny pleaded as they pressed closer to him. The sucker feigned laughter but they could sense his panic. "I can smell your fear, dreg." The smile drained from the sucker's face as he glanced up at Lanny.

"Do it." Luca said as he stepped backwards.

"Ad infernum rubigo." Shouted Lanny as he turned in a three sixty and the blade of his broadsword connected cleanly with the vampire and the sucker's head severed from his shoulders. He enjoyed sending them to the Tenth.

The head rolled onto the floor and Bjorn kicked it in disgust, over to the fallen body and they stepped away as the light turned the form to dust as his energy left his body and was now imprisoned in the tenth dimension.

"How did you know it wasn't the leader?" Peo asked as he stared at Lanny, as they wiped their blades.

"I didn't." Lanny admitted and grinned at them when he saw their expressions. "At least not until I smelt his fear." He laughed raucously at the look of disbelief written on their faces.

"One of these days, Jarl, that sense of smell you credit so much, will let you down." Bjorn said laughing as they made their way back out into the passageway.

They walked back along the way they had come, and Lanny nodded at the staircase. It led down to another level. Bjorn and Lanny carefully descended the steps and as they walked along the darkened pathway, the heard the vampires arguing as they awakened. He grinned to himself.

Carefully the two Militibus walked along with their backs close to the walls. At the end of the passage, Lanny glanced at Bjorn and in seconds, they had burst into the room and beheaded four of the hoods.

Two other suckers retreated out to the void beyond. Seeing this, Lanny ran after them and as he entered the room, he threw the axe at the head of the creature and as he fell, Lanny ran and picked up his axe and beheaded the dreg.

As Lanny was standing up, he felt arms grab him from behind and as he tried to free himself from their grip, he heard the unmistakable swishing sound of the mace. He threw the criminal who had tried to imprison him away from him and with a flash of his sword he cleanly severed the head. *Scum!* Lanny felt filthy now. He hated this part of the hunt.

"You OK, Jarl?" Bjorn asked and Lanny nodded, and they hurried over to the door at the end of the room and Bjorn kicked it open and ran inside.

"Letting your scum soldiers do your killing for you." Lanny roared as he came into the centre of the room. "Typical of you, blood trash. Afraid." Bjorn agreed and laughed loudly as they went over to the bed where the leader was sitting up, still half asleep.

"I heard you upstairs, Militibus." He said but as he tried to get up, Lanny extended his arm and pressed his sword against the vamp's throat. "Go ahead, but your leader will not be happy with you, if you kill me." The predator laughed and Lanny saw the broken fang. He knew then that he wasn't an alpha, just the leader of the omegas in the lair.

"Berserker, go get the Praetorian and the General." Lanny ordered without taking his eyes off the sucker.

"Yes sir." Bjorn said and hurriedly left the room.

"So, the berserker does what he is told like a good little bitch." The vampire laughed loudly, and Lanny pressed the blade a little harder onto his throat. "I finally get to meet the famous Tempus Militibus. Can't say that I'm impressed." He goaded.

"It will give me great pleasure to finish you off, sucker." Lanny shrieked at him and stepped away when he heard the others enter the room.

"The pleasure will be mine," the vampire said and stared at Luca. "Which one of you is the lead bitch?" He laughed at his own joke and the bed shook with his weight.

"I thought, a vampire leader would be more..." Luca looked at him with disdain. "Terrifying." The three Militibus sniggered as they glared at the sucker in the bed.

"So, what can I do for you, General?" He asked, looking amused at the Militibus standing in his quarters.

"Who hired you?" Luca asked him as he walked over to the door and closed it firmly behind him. The sucker heaved with laughter.

"You expect me to tell you that?" He shook his head and laughed louder. "You must be lacking in oxygen if you think I will tell you anything, even if you are Militibus." Lanny stepped forward and with the side of his axe he lashed out at the dreg.

"We know someone hired you to frighten the residents of the hotel." Luca said as he stood at the foot of the bed and glared at the pale overweight bloodsucker. "Why?"

"You know nothing, you sanctimonious prick." The sucker shouted and chuckled as he glared back at the Militibus.

"It would be in your best interest to answer my questions." Luca said unaffected by the outburst. He nodded at Bjorn, who moved to the right side of the bed and pulled on the arm of the sucker as Peo stepped forward with his silver dagger and sliced off the vampire's index finger. "Now, tell me, who hired you and why?" Luca repeated, without breaking into a sweat, but the sucker just laughed and refused to answer.

Lanny stood up straight and looked across at his commander and then back at the vampire. "I ain't afraid of the pretty boy here." The street scum retorted and spat out onto the floor.

"You should be." Lanny said as he raised the axe and hit him on the side of the face with the flat side of the instrument. "You see, sucker, unlike my friends here, I enjoy the torture that I will mete out to you." Lanny sneered at him. "Believe me."

"Make it easy on yourself you filthy leech." Peo said as he cut another finger off. "The feeding you did last will soon be drained and you will become anaemic, fair game for the strigoi."

"You think I fear the strigoi? I don't." The sucker hissed at him angrily, but his eyes belied his bravado.

"You have been given enough time to answer." Luca declared and stood up straight. "Jarl, he's all yours." Lanny grinned and raised the axe above his head and as it was about to come down on the sucker, the scumbag cried out.

"Alright." Lanny slung the axe in his hand and laughed at him. "I don't know his name." Lanny raised the axe once more. "But there was an older man with him." The vampire said hurriedly now.

"Who was in charge?" Luca asked.

"The small fat man. He didn't speak but he was the one in control." The sucker said. "The older man told me to bring my nest here and do whatever it took to get the drunks out."

"Where did you meet him?" Luca asked sternly.

"He came to a bar in the Nevada desert, a disused movie set." The thug snarled. "There was payment of a hundred thousand dollars to be given as a bonus on top of the hundred grand already paid if we did it by the end of the renovations and before the rest moved in." The vampire looked at the Militibus.

"Did you get a name?" Bjorn asked and the sucker just laughed as he looked at him.

"He called him John." The punk said and Lanny looked at Luca.

"The quiet one," Lanny turned back to the criminal, "was he the owner of the building?" The sucker laughed and nodded. "Did you see him again?"

"No but I am to meet with both of them on Saturday to get the rest of my money." The creature just grinned at him, and Lanny could see the brown blood stains on his teeth.

"Where is this meeting to take place?" Lanny bellowed.

"You expect me to tell you that?" He asked and Lanny raised the axe again. "OK, OK, it's to take place at a bar in a hotel." He grinned at the Jarl.

"Sucker, you think we are stupid or something?" Lanny said in a serious tone. "I'll be with you, I believe you that there is a meeting, but guess what?" Lanny leered at him. "I don't believe it's in a hotel, so if you could try and remember where it will really be held, I can get on with my day, or I will enjoy sending you to Gehenna." Lanny smiled at him. He was enjoying seeing the dreg suffer now.

"You're insane if you think I'm telling you lies." The sucker protested. "I'm telling you the truth... you have to believe me." He sounded desperate now, but Lanny didn't believe him.

"Then I guess either way you don't get your piece of the pie, sucker." Lanny said and grinned. "Because I know you are lying." The vampire looked at Luca, but Luca just grinned at him.

"You call off this lunatic." He begged and looked towards the Jarl and Lanny smiled as he smelt his fear. But it was fear of the Militibus that filled him with dread, nothing more.

"Unfortunately, for you," Luca said with a grin. "Unless you level with me, the Jarl will be uncontrollable." Lanny scorned as he looked at the sucker and raised his eyebrows and shook his head. He wore a sarcastic expression, which told the dreg he was going to die either way.

"OK, I'm supposed to get a call and then meet with the mort's, top of the hotel." The leader said. "I'm expected there alone. Just me and the two blood banks."

"Thank you for being so cooperative." Luca said and began to walk away followed by Bjorn and Peo.

Lanny laughed as he looked at the sucker lying on the bed. "Requiem in inferno rubigo." He raised the axe and brought it down hard on his neck. His head was severed cleanly, and Lanny picked it up and threw it on the bed on top of the lead vampire of the lair.

Chapter 18

Lanny turned off the faucet and wrapped the towel around his waist. He hated having the smell of suckers' stench on him. It made him feel dirty.

He walked into the bedroom and opened the door of the large wardrobe. He picked out a white silk shirt and a dark pants and brought them over to the bed and laid them out on it. Lanny threw the towel onto the floor and looked at the clothes on the bed. He was looking forward to relaxing for the evening at Bjorn's club. It had been an exhilarating experience, toying with the sucker.

Lanny dressed quickly and brushed his long blond hair. He was a handsome man, with his ice blue eyes, framed with long dark lashes. His chiselled nose and high cheek bones were typically Nordic. He splashed on some cologne and took out his jacket from the wardrobe. Lanny approved of his choice of clothing. He liked the feel and the cut of the designer suit that he wore.

He walked into the lounge and picked up his phone and car keys. As he was leaving the penthouse, his phone rang.

"Hello." He said nonchalantly as he made sure he had everything that he needed.

"Mr Lancnut...Lanny?" He smiled to himself.

"Sister Angelica, what can I do for you?" He asked her carefully. He could hear her breathe. It was a beautiful sound. He liked the sound of her breathing. It filled him with an excitement, an exhilaration of sorts.

"I don't mean to disturb you, and I know you are very busy." She faltered and he could hear the uncertainty in her voice. This intrigued him.

"I'm not busy at all." Lanny lied and smiled to himself once more. "What can I do for you?" He asked her again.

"I heard what Father O'Hara said to you." She muttered almost in a whisper. "He didn't mean it, believe me, he has been..." He heard the suffering in her tone too.

"Sister Angelica, are you free right now?" Lanny asked her quickly, he really wanted to see her.

"Yes, I'm on my way to the soup kitchen." She mumbled. "Why?"

"I'll meet you there." Lanny blurted out; he was now smiling widely.

"OK." She said and he hung up.

Lanny drove quickly and through several red lights. He didn't care, he was keen to see her. He had to be with her, even for a few stolen minutes of her time.

As he pulled up near the soup kitchen, he saw the nun. She was standing on the corner, and she appeared nervous, unsure of herself. This made him smile even more as her whole demeanour echoed her shyness and yet he found this devastatingly attractive. Usually he liked his females confident, self-assured and decisive, everything that Sister Angelica was not.

Lanny opened the door and got out of the car and walked with long strides over to where the nun stood. He called out her name and she turned to him. Lanny grinned at her and nervously she returned his smile.

"I didn't mean to interrupt your evening." She said as she glanced at him in his designer suit. He saw her blush.

"You didn't." Lanny reassured her with a smile. "Do you have time for a cup of coffee?" She nodded and he led her over to his car. He drove out of skid row and back the way he had come. He didn't want to talk to her, where there was a chance, they would be interrupted by the priest or some other nuns. All trying to protect her virtue from him.

"Have you eaten?" Lanny asked suddenly as he glanced across at her. She had her hands clasped together and rested on her lap. She was all tightened up in a ball of nervous energy.

"No, not until after I finish work at the mission tonight." Sister Angelica replied.

"Is there someone else working with you?" Lanny asked her quickly.

"Yes, Sister Maud and Sister Regina." She spoke. "I volunteered to go help tonight. I'm not really needed there." Lanny smiled at her, he had needed to hear that.

"In that case," he said firmly. "I'll take you to dinner." She shook her head strongly in protest, but Lanny just smirked at her, dismissing all her objections.

He picked up his phone and dialled the number. "Bjorn, I'm busy and may be late."

"What? Why?" Bjorn quizzed and Lanny could tell he was smiling.

"Later Berserker." Lanny chuckled and hung up. He looked over at the nun she looked shy and very beautiful. He was getting stiff.

Lanny pulled the car into the parking lot and turned off the engine. He glanced at her briefly. "Do you like Mexican?" He asked her. She nodded. "This is a nice restaurant, you'll like it." He got out followed by the nun.

Lanny walked ahead of her, and opened the door, and he stood aside and held it for her.

They were seated in a dark corner and the waiter handed them their menus.

When they had ordered he asked the waiter to bring them a bottle of 2001 cabernet sauvignon. When he was gone, Sister Angelica smiled nervously at him.

"This is a nice place." She said and he simpered as she looked around. "I've never been to a place like this before." She giggled. "Do you come here a lot?"

"Your faith doesn't allow you to eat out?" Lanny asked as the waiter poured a little wine into the glass, and he took a sip. He nodded and the waiter poured the nun a glass.

"No, my vocation doesn't allow me to have dinner with a man." Lanny looked into her green eyes. He was enchanted by her.

"You have dinner with the padre?" Lanny confirmed. "He's a man." He delighted in her conflict.

"He's not a man...not like you are." She stammered and Lanny beamed at her as she struggled to condone having dinner with a member of the opposite sex. He was really enjoying her company.

"it's just dinner, Sister." He reassured her. "You called me for a reason." He looked into her face.

"Father O'Hara said some awful things to you and to Mr Meridian." She spoke softly. "He called you both names, dreadful names." The waiter passed their table with two plates for the customers sitting a couple of tables away from theirs. Lanny observed the action as he listened to her.

"Yes, he did." Lanny affirmed and lifted the glass to his mouth and took a sip of the blood red wine. "He was upset. I understand that" He could sense the nun's assumed betrayal of the padre and her vocation.

"He has been stressed out lately by these deaths and now poor Grace," the nun said as she looked at him with wide eyes. "Father O'Hara is a good man." She said sadly.

"I know he is." Lanny agreed. "Tell me Sister..." The waiter looked at the nun briefly and then at Lanny as he placed their order in front of them. "The padre, is he a true believer?"

"A true believer?" She queried and she looked confused, as her body language gave her away.

"He argued that the businessmen that he is doing business with are good men," Lanny said as he took a forkful of rice. "Does he truly believe that?" He studied her expression carefully. He heard her heart beating fast but it wasn't because she was being untruthful, she was tormented by her feelings of desire.

"Father O'Hara believes there is good in everyone." Sister Angelica said as he looked at her. "Mr...Lanny." She was nervous again and he could hear it in her voice. "He called you murderers and... vampires...are you?" Her voice was shaky, even though she tried hard to disguise it.

"Am I a murderer or a vampire?" He teased the nun. "Which do you think?" She stared at him, unsure of what to answer. Lanny snorted at this. "Sister Angelica, I am not a murderer. I am just a man who likes to help people who have been wronged. Like aiding your priest with this project." She looked at him, shyly again, she seemed relieved.

"You won't cancel the cheque then?" Sister Angelica looked concerned, and Lanny laughed loudly.

"Sister, I won't cancel the cheque so you can reassure the padre," he said with a grin. "He won't get rid of the Militibus that easily." She gazed at him. "We will finish our investigation and bring it to a conclusion." He reassured her.

"Militibus? That's the name of your investigative company?" She asked. "That means warrior, doesn't it?"

"You speak Latin?" He asked amused, but he was interested.

"I'm a nun, of course I speak Latin." She smiled warmly at him. He couldn't deny that she was arousing feelings he had thought were long buried but she was off limits, and off limits to him because of her innocence.

"Tell me some more about you, Sister." He asked her in a serious tone. Lanny was curious about her, and he wanted to know more.

"I'm not very interesting." She protested and lowered her eyes. She lacked so much confidence in herself. She was a wallflower.

"Oh, but you are, Sister." He admitted and smiled. "What is your real name?"

"Adeline." She replied after a moment. "But I haven't been called that in such a long time." Her voice trailed off as if in a reverie.

"It's a very beautiful name." Lanny said and looked into her eyes, but she lowered her head. "Why don't you look at me?" He asked her in his baritone voice.

"I find you very intense when you look at me the way that you are now." She replied honestly.

"Is that the only reason?" He probed, and he could hear the change in her heartbeat. He wondered if it had anything to do with the attraction that she felt toward him.

"You are a very handsome man." She admitted. "But I can't see you that way so it's better not to look at you at all." He smiled widely at her. So, underneath the indoctrination of her vows, she still possessed human feelings after all, and was prone to emotions like desire, even if she did suppress it. Lanny was amused.

"You are very beautiful, Adeline." Lanny said and reached out to touch her hand with his finger. "Incredibly beautiful." She pulled her hand away.

"Don't...don't you have a wife or someone special?" She stammered a little and took a gulp of wine to steady her nerves.

"I'm not married." Lanny said in a low tone. "There hasn't been anyone special in my life for a long, long time." She looked up at him, she seemed almost relieved by his confession.

"I'm sorry." She whispered.

"Waiter, the bill." Lanny called to the passing waiter without looking up. "I'll take you home." He said and smiled at her once more. He didn't want her to feel uncomfortable, he knew she was now, that she had unintentionally revealed her desire for him and in any other circumstances he would gladly take advantage of the situation.

They walked slowly to his car, and he opened the door for her, and she got in. Lanny sniffed the air, it smelled stale, like death. There was a dreg nearby. He opened the door and got in.

He drove Sister Angelica back to the convent where she lived. Lanny stopped the car and turned off the engine. He turned to her and said gently. "Thank you for having dinner with me." He reached over and kissed her softly on the cheek. "You are a good woman, Adeline." She looked up into his eyes and he heard her catch her breath and he could sense her shiver. Lanny wanted to kiss her, and he knew that she wanted him too as well. What harm would a kiss be? He wondered.

"Tha...thank you." She opened the door and stepped out of the car but before she closed it, she looked at him. "I can't imagine why you have no one to love in your life." She closed the door, and quickly walked away. Lanny watched her as she walked up the steps of the convent and went inside.

I could love you! He thought to himself.

Then he hurriedly drove out of the convent yard and back out onto the road.

Chapter 19

Father O'Hara stood up and turned to look at the man standing in the middle of the library. He was small in stature and rather stout, his dark hair was coloured to disguise the greys which by now would be his permanent colouring. His eyes were cold as steel as they squinted at Tom and his mannerisms hard and accusatory in nature.

Tom couldn't believe the accusation from his superior. *The nerve of the man!*

"Furthermore, O'Hara, you seem that have lost control of your charge and those under your care." He swung around and stared at the man before him. He was doing his best, but he couldn't control what was happening at the hotel. No one could, he couldn't be held accountable for that.

There was a doubt now in the back of his mind whether he had been too hasty in dismissing the vampires as he had, but he certainly couldn't tell his bishop he had been conversing with predators, he'd surely have him dismissed and committed for madness. He felt he was slowly going insane. The stress was becoming too much for him.

"Bishop Corkery," Father O'Hara said in his soft lilt. "Sister Angelica is a devout nun, she certainly has no interest in mortal man, only in God." He knew of course, who the man was, that the young nun had been out with. It was the blond Militibus officer Lanny Lancnut. He was sure it was innocent, at least on the part of the nun. He couldn't say with any certainty about the vampire.

He wasn't blind, Tom had seen how the vampire looked at the young nun. He had seen the lust in his eyes. "The young man in question I don't know personally but I do know Sister Angelica." He partially lied and rubbed his forehead aggressively with his right hand, a habit he had picked up in the seminary when he felt stressed out over exams.

"I demand that you keep her away from the soup kitchen, O'Hara," Bishop Corkery said angrily, and Tom noticed that his nostrils flared like a horse. "I will make the necessary arrangements to have that nun removed to another convent as far from temptation as possible." Tom stared at him. What the bishop intended doing was preposterous. He didn't know Sister Angelica, she wasn't like what he was suggesting, throwing herself in the way of temptation. The very idea of it was ludicrous. It was unfair to punish her for the vampire's lustful thoughts.

"That would kill her, these people are her life's work." Father O'Hara begged on behalf of his young nun. "They depend on her too." *I depend on her!* He thought to himself.

"Any luck convincing the drunks about moving into the hotel?" The bishop asked quickly changing the subject. Father O'Hara stared at him for a moment. He knew his bishop was angry with him but there was no reason to belittle the residents of the hotel. No reason at all. Corkery showed no Christian charity whatsoever.

"They have concerns, and fears have been raised by some people." He said honestly. "But they are eager to move and get off the street."

"I hope so, for your sake, O'Hara," Corkery advised bitterly. "If they don't I understand the building will be repurposed for other use. That would be unfortunate, for you." He walked over to the door and opened it, then he turned around and said in a serious tone. "If you don't succeed consider it your passport to Honduras." He left the room without closing the door.

Bishop Corkery passed two men as he made his way to his Mercedes. He was livid with O'Hara; the man was so bloody minded and stubborn. One of the men hit against him and mumbled something that he didn't understand, he opened his car but before he got in, he puzzled for a moment, then he shook his head, got in and drove away.

*****

Luca watched the car drive away and turned to Lanny and said casually. "Did you sense that?" The Jarl nodded. "Who is he? He seems...familiar." But Luca just shrugged it off and they walked on.

"I'm sure the padre will tell us." Lanny answered disinterestedly as they climbed the steps and rang the bell. But he looked after the car as it drove away. Lanny too was perturbed by the man they had just encountered.

The door was opened by the housekeeper who welcomed them in her usual warm way, and they were shown into the library. "Father O'Hara, you called us here." Luca said as he shook hands with the priest. He looked at Lanny distrustfully, but he shook hands with him reluctantly.

"Who was that, just now?" Lanny blurted out, in true Jarl style, and without waiting for the pleasantries to be out of the way.

"That was Bishop Corkery." Father O'Hara replied and showed his displeasure with the Jarl. "You have some explaining to do young man." He said angrily to Lanny, who just smirked back at him, riling the priest by neither admitting nor denying what he was about to be accused of.

"Do I?" He asked mischievously, playing with the priest. He enjoyed the effect that he had on him.

"You have no right in trying to romance an innocent young woman." Lanny raised an eyebrow in feigned shock at such a suggestion. Luca looked from the priest to Lanny and saw him smile.

"What's going on Jarl?" He asked carefully and watched as Lanny walked over to the window and glanced outside and then he looked back at them and then he became serious.

"Yes, Sister Angelica had dinner with me the other night." Lanny said curtly and directed his gaze toward the priest. "She went to great trouble to convince me, you were worth helping, padre." Lanny smiled and Luca could sense that it was more than he let on. "I'm afraid I need more convincing because I think you just want to trade insults with me. You don't care so long as she doesn't have dinner with a man."

"Sister Angelica has her habit," Father O'Hara said angrily. "She is forbidden to mortal man."

"I'm not a mortal man, though am I padre?" Luca suppressed a smile. Lanny had a wicked sense of humour, and he enjoyed his petty quarrel with the priest. That much was obvious. "The sister is troubled and concerned about the residents, she has no interest in romance, or sex, so relax. She is trained well." The priest inhaled sharply.

"Bishop Corkery saw you with her, he tells a very different tale, indeed." Father O'Hara insisted grimly as he glared back at him but Lanny laughed raucously at this.

"Jarl, enough of your game." Luca stepped in and turned to the priest. "Father O'Hara, we spoke with the sucker who was hired by someone from your circle." The priest stared at him indignantly.

"What are you saying?" He demanded gingerly.

"They were hired so the housing project would fail." Lanny confirmed as he walked over to the fireplace and placed his left leg on the hearth. "Now, we need to know who on the committee is called John?"

"You met him, John Josess, he's the building contractor but he's a good man." Father O'Hara said heatedly and glared at them. "There's no way I can believe that he would hire...vampires." He looked troubled as he said it.

"You would vouch for him?" Luca asked. The priest nodded hesitantly. "Anyone else that you would know who is called John?" He shook his head.

"Of course, the dreg could be lying, General." Lanny revealed and then he looked at the priest. "I sent him to the Tenth dimension." He declared deliberately indifferent. "So, we won't know now."

"God have mercy on his soul." Father O'Hara muttered and quickly blessed himself.

"He was responsible for the deaths of your parishioners, padre." Lanny bellowed at him. "So don't pray over that scum." The clergyman stared at him, shocked by the power of his voice, by the power of what he was.

"Lanny, go wait in the car." Luca said as he diffused the situation, it was spiralling out of control fast. Lanny was a hothead and the priest just seemed to vex him.

He watched as Lanny walked over to the door and opened it and left. When they were alone, Luca turned to the priest and asked assertively. "It's important, to know who this John is, he was with the owner of the building when they hired the criminals." Luca said a little more gently now and walked over to the old man. "I know you don't like us, and Lanny certainly has got your back up, but Father O'Hara for the sake of those people, that you are trying to help, tell me what you know." Luca put his hand gently on his shoulder. "We want to assist you in this, bring justice to those people living on the street." Father O'Hara looked at him. Luca could see the troubled look in his eyes, the weight of the burden he felt for not being able to house everyone.

"Would you like a sherry?" Tom asked suddenly and then added. "Can you drink, like us?" Luca smiled widely at him.

"A sherry would be nice." He nodded. "We are able to do all the things a mortal can do, with just a few exceptions." The priest laughed fretfully and filled two glasses with his favourite Spanish sherry.

"What about Lanny? Should we invite him back inside?" Father O'Hara inquired gently. Luca grinned, shook his head, and said as he took the glass from the priest.

"The Jarl can cool off first." They both laughed, the atmosphere lightened between them now. "He is a good man, Father, you can trust him." Luca added honestly. "I trust him implicitly, with my life."

"You must forgive me, Mr Meridian, as I know nothing about how to deal with vampires." Father O'Hara said. "Your existence was unknown to me until a few weeks ago."

"We are not like the suckers, hired to jeopardise your project." Luca said. "We are Tempus Militibus, we don't live off human blood, as you think we do."

"Tempus Militibus," Father O'Hara repeated. "Time Warriors." Luca nodded with a slow smile on his handsome face.

"Yes, we are the elite from the Sixth dimension, aligned here to right wrongs that are visited on the innocent in this dimension, by the dregs who escape from other realms." Luca said, he believed in the code that they lived by. "Now, it would be helpful if you could tell me about this John, if it isn't Josess, who could it be?"

"If I knew I would tell you." The priest replied in a serious tone. "I can only say that when the negotiation took place for the hotel, I wasn't at it but there was a man representing the committee, you met him the other day." Luca looked at him. "Jonah Moriarty, he was there on behalf of the committee, but I don't believe he would do such a thing."

"Where does he work or live?" Luca enquired carefully.

"He works as treasurer for us, he's the bishop's private secretary." Father O'Hara said, and appeared lost in thought as he scratched his head with his right hand. "I can call him here for Friday if it's that important."

"It is," Luca said and stood up. "Don't let him know what it's about, I'll send the Berserker, to talk with you and him, that way he won't suspect us, as he hasn't met Bjorn before." They shook hands and Luca walked over to the door. "Talk soon

Father." He smiled and left the library and walked out of the house and over to the car and got in.

"You took your time." Lanny said huffily.

"I had sherry with the padre." Luca advised sarcastically as Lanny drove away.

"So, you are best friends already." Lanny said sulkily and Luca just laughed. "That didn't take long."

"He's a very interesting man," Luca reposted with a wicked grin. "You should try being less hostile, Jarl." Lanny muttered something in his native dialect and Luca just roared with laughter at the childishness of the Jarl.

Chapter 20

The man holding the Ming vase was studying it carefully. He turned it over and looked at it from different angles. It was obvious that he was no expert.

Lanny observed from the security monitors in his office. He had seen the man before. It was the contractor for the hotel, John Josess. His interest was aroused now as to why this man was in his store.

Lanny stood up and buttoned the top button of his black designer suit. He walked unhurriedly over to the door, opened it and walked into the shop.

He smiled widely as he walked over to the contractor. "Hello again." Lanny greeted as he held out his hand to him. He both disliked and distrusted him but he would remain as charming as he could with him.

"Well, hello, again." John Josess said shaking his hand, he appeared nervous. "So, this is what you do is it?" He looked around and his mouth was pressed tight as he took in the impressive store. "It's not what I was expecting." Josess nodded, he was fascinated by the antiques.

"What were you expecting?" Lanny asked with a grin. "A dark dingy place selling replicas?" Josess laughed nervously. He was twitching and Lanny sensed that he was a naturally nervous man but with the line of business he was in, nervousness was not an advantage.

"No...I don't know...you're a young man." He said after a moment and offered a tense grin.

"Age is but a number, Mr Josess." Lanny replied with a certain diplomacy as he watched him put the vase carefully back on its stand. "Now, what can I do for you?" Lanny observed indifferently, as he listened to the quickening of Josess heartbeat.

"I wanted…" He dabbed his neck. He was sweating and then he fixed his tie. The man was a wreck.

"You wanted?" Lanny probed, secretly he was enjoying his torture. *Parasite!* He thought to himself, but he kept his poker face and Josess was unaware of Lanny's real mood.

"I wanted to talk with you." Josess said regaining his composure. "If you have time, that is." Lanny flashed him a brilliant smile and motioned for the contractor to follow him.

He led him to his office and asked if he would like a drink. "It's not too early, is it?" Josess asked as he tried to remain focussed, something that Lanny sensed would be difficult for a man like Josess.

"Where I come from its happy hour right now." Lanny said as Josess laughed.

"Whiskey then," Josess said greedily. "Where are you from Mr Lancnut?" Lanny poured the drinks and handed a glass to him.

"Denmark," Lanny replied and sat down behind his large desk and studied his guest intently. He knew his type, wary at first, then became comfortable before revealing his true intention. Lanny didn't like his type, he was dirty and although he did try to hide it, he wasn't succeeding.

"This is good whiskey." John Josess broke the silence, he appeared to be nervous again. "You speak very good English, hardly an accent at all, well maybe just a hint." He commented and averted his eyes away. His type could never look one straight in the eye.

"Mr Josess, with respect but you didn't come here to discuss my language capability, now what can I do for you?" Lanny was beginning to bore with the encounter already. "I do have certain business to attend."

"You're right, forgive me." Josess said as he placed the glass on the desk. "Frank...Rostern and I were wondering how...that is, why a rich young man like yourself wanted to invest in the hotel in skid row." Lanny knew that he was lying, his heartbeat quickened when he lied or was uncomfortable. His pulse was racing, and he could hear the blood course through his veins. This man was a liability in every sense. It would be foolish to trust him, for under the right circumstances he would talk just to save his own neck.

"It's a good cause, and I enjoy a good cause, besides..." Lanny averred after a moment. "I have some money lying idle, so why not?" He smiled widely at him as Josess shifted anxiously in his seat, it was obvious that he didn't want to be there, but he was chosen to go, to suss out the Jarl. To get information that might be suitable for their own ends.

"Are you...Umm...are you still looking for an investment?" John Josess dithered as he reached for the glass. "A good investment." *There, it was out at last!* Lanny thought to himself.

"That would depend on what I would be investing in." Lanny played it cool, but he was still smiling.

"Well Frank...Frank and I have, along with..." He faltered and he was sweating profusely now. "We have a very rich silent partner, and we have some luxury condos coming...coming on stream shortly." Lanny sat back in his seat and looked intently at him. He didn't like him. This man was slime, with a capitol 'S'.

"Go on." Lanny encouraged, from across the desk.

"We hope...we hope to have the...um...renovations beginning in a couple of weeks." Josess pursued erratically. "A small investment from yourself, Mr Lancnut, will yield you millions of dollars."

"Where is the building located?" Lanny quizzed but he already knew the answer.

"All in good time, Mr Lancnut." Josess said a little more bravely now. "Are you interested?" Lanny leaned forward and looked him flush in the eyes. Josess lowered his gaze away from Lanny's, he couldn't look at him.

"How much are we talking about?" Lanny asked him seriously. "Both in investment and return?" He saw Josess smile slowly once more, and Lanny knew that the older man assumed that he had just snared a new investor.

"Twenty million, return." He was beside himself now with excitement. Lanny sensed the adrenaline, and he smelled the pheromones as they excreted their sickening scent.

"How many investors?" Lanny probed carefully. "Surely the more investors there are, it would lessen the return on investment?" He looked as though he was hooked now.

"If you came on board, Mr Lancnut," he was grinning wildly now. "There would be four, including you."

"Why would you want me on board, Mr Josess, you don't know me?" Lanny said as he took a sip from the glass in his hand. "Do you invite anyone you meet because you assume they have money?"

"No, that's true I...we don't know you, but" Josess said as he leaned forward. "We can offer you a better investment than the priest. His, is all take whereas ours is giving back to you, more than what you invest." It was obvious that he was greedy and that there wasn't any level which he wouldn't stoop to, to make money. He reeked of corruption. But Lanny wondered just what his role was in the scheme? It was clear he was the errand boy, as Rostern hadn't deemed himself lowly enough to seek out Lanny for the purpose to incite him to part with millions of dollars in their Ponzi scheme.

"If I were to agree," Lanny asked. "Where would I be investing?" He studied him and as he did, he saw that the question made Josess rather uncomfortable. Lanny smirked at this.

"On skid row." John Josess replied but he quickly added. "There are big plans to clean it up." He lied. A long slow smile spread across Lanny's handsome face. He didn't even have to try hard to snare Josess.

"I would want to meet this silent investor." He said and put his glass down. "If I were to invest anything."

"That would be difficult to arrange." Josess replied a little too quickly.

"Then I couldn't-"

"But it's not impossible." Josess quickly cut him off. Lanny stood up and held out his hand to him. "Nothing is impossible, right, Mr Lancnut?"

"In that case, Mr Josess," Lanny said walking him back out into the shop. "We may have a deal, if the terms are favourable to me." They shook hands and Lanny watched him leave the store.

When Josess was gone, Lanny took out his phone and called Luca.

Chapter 21

"This is insanity, Lanny." Peo raised his voice as he watched the Viking pace up and down in the penthouse lounge. "I don't think you have given this much thought." Peo gaped at him.

"Peo is right, Lanny." Bjorn joined in. "You don't know if it's a trap to draw you out." Lanny just smiled at his friends. Of course, they were right it may well be a ruse to lure him out. Maybe the 'Silent investor' knows he is a vampire and has laid a trap to expose him. Either way, it was worth a shot. They didn't have much else to go on, did they?

"Look, if there was another way, I'd use that." Lanny informed them as he glanced over at Luca for affirmation that he was right, but he didn't see anything in Luca's expression to support him. "The priest, already mistrusts me, so it's a good cover." Lanny didn't see it as something that he couldn't handle.

"What if they have suckers lying in wait for you?" Peo pointed out. There were times when the two Militibus went head-to-head and ended up in a skirmish, but they always had each other's back. "At least, if we shadowed you, Jarl, and you needed us, we are there."

"Peo, that's the point, if you were discovered, our cover is blown, and the mission has failed." Lanny pleaded. "This way, I size up this silent investor and we can expose the whole fraud." He glanced across at Luca once more. "If Josess is anything to go by, it could very well be nothing more than a group of idiots trying to get rich quick." He was trying hard and failing to convince his friends of what he had decided to do.

"General, will you tell him, that it's madness to go alone." Bjorn implored in an exasperated tone. Lanny looked across at his commander. His deportment was steadfast.

"I think the Jarl is right." Luca agreed after a while, and a smile spread across Lanny's face. "But you won't be alone, Jarl, we will be close by." Luca said tenaciously. "You will attend the meeting alone. We won't interfere unless we sense the need to."

"They have gone mad." Peo called out exasperated and walked over to where Lanny stood. He put his hand on Lanny's arm. "At least take a weapon." He pleaded earnestly.

"No, look if it is discovered, my cover is blown." Lanny said in an ominous tone. "Then there is no use in us fighting for justice for those misfortunate people." All three of the Militibus stared at him simultaneously. Lanny had been against the idea from the beginning, and he knew that he had been wrong, his own vanity had gotten in the way of what their purpose in the Fourth dimension was. And now, as he had mulled it over in his mind, following conversations with the nun, and with the padre too, Lanny was now on the side of the residents. He certainly was a complex creature.

"OK, we will be waiting in Luca's SUV across from the bar," Peo said reluctantly, but it was obvious he didn't agree with the plan. "At least have them sit at the window, so we can observe." Lanny grinned at him and slapped him on the arm.

"I didn't know you cared, Praetorian?" They both laughed loudly. "It's so touching." Then Lanny walked over to the door and turned to his comrades. "I'll see you Friday evening then." He left.

*****

Father O'Hara sat down beside the fireplace and was trying to read a book. It had been a troublesome time for him lately. He had had his bishop call on him twice since and he had informed him that he had written to the mother superior about Sister Angelica's cavorting with a strange man. Father O'Hara didn't want to admit to Bishop Corkery, that the young man in question wasn't really a man at all but how could he broach a subject like that? Tom's main concern was that Sister Angelica remain at the convent. She was needed there and besides she was innocent. He really didn't believe that she would allow herself to fall into the clutches of an immoral creature, like the vampire, would she? Tom shook his head. He was being preposterous again. This whole affair with the hotel, the bishop and the vampires were driving him into a ball of stress.

He knew the nun's work was exemplary and that there was no cause for alarm regarding her vocation. But he wondered about the vampire. After all, what did he know of the Militibus? Nothing. He had placed his trust in a group of vigilantes that he knew nothing about. *Dangerous vampires!*

He felt tired. He felt harassed and he didn't know how he would find a way out of his predicament. *Was there really any hope?* Tom knew that he had to rid himself of this negativity, if he didn't, what use was he to anyone?

The door opened and the young nun came in with a cup and saucer in her hand. She was humming a tune. "I thought you might enjoy a cup of cocoa, Father." Sister Angelica said as she left the cup on the coffee table.

"Thank you, child." He spoke softly to her. "Can you sit and chat for a while?"

"I have to be at the soup kitchen shortly." She said in her cheery voice. "Is there something troubling you, Father?" She asked, she wore a look of concern as she glanced at the priest. He felt guilty now, for doubting her.

"No, child." He spoke. "I'll come down and help you tonight. It will be nice to talk to some of those waiting for shelter." She smiled fondly at him and left the library. But Father O'Hara, felt disappointed with himself again, that the real reason he was going to the soup kitchen wasn't to converse with his flock but to keep an eye on the nun in case the vampire tried to lure her away in his car. *The vampire!* How could he even come to terms with that? How could he fight against that?

Father O'Hara didn't drink the cocoa, he stood up and went out into the hallway and put on his blazer and walked back into the library and put his book back on the shelf and returned to the hall and left the parochial house to go to the soup kitchen.

He had to get out of the house. But it was more a case that he had to spy, wasn't it? He thought harshly to himself.

Chapter 22

Bjorn and Peo had reconnoitred an area in skid row. The residents of tent city were on edge tonight, and they were restless. *Scared!*

Neither of the Militibus spoke as they walked, each were lost in their own thoughts but what was playing on both their minds was the crazy plan that Lanny had conjured up concerning the contractor John Josess, and to inform him that he was in, regarding the luxury condos.

No amount of discussion would change the Jarl's mind. He was determined to go ahead with it regardless of what they said. It was madness. Something was up with him, something besides the case they were working.

"It seems quiet tonight." Peo commented, almost miserably. Bjorn glanced at him.

"For how long, though?" Bjorn was always suspicious about nights like this. He didn't like it when it got too quiet, it usually meant that something was about to happen, and it wouldn't be good either.

"I don't think anything will go down tonight, not here." Peo stated as he glanced over at the two men huddled around the burning barrel. They were getting warmth into their hands as they held them close to the flame.

Just then, Bjorn stopped, and his nostrils flared. "What is it?" Peo asked as he too stopped in his tracks and sniffed the air.

"Do you smell that?" Bjorn whispered in a low tone, Peo nodded and looked over to where the two men were warming their hands. They were now joined by a third man who was looking over at them. "He's a sucker." Bjorn stated and put his hand inside his jacket and felt for the handle of the mace. He was ready for action.

"He knows what we are too." Peo said and was prepared with his dagger. "Let's not give him cause to come over." Bjorn agreed and they walked on but at a quicker pace. Vigilant about their surroundings now, but not wanting to draw attention either. Not that night, anyway.

As they rounded the corner, they were met by four bloodsuckers. They were grinning when they saw the Militibus.

"You are out of your usual throughfare." One of the vampire's said with an aggressive tone. "We don't like the Militibus round here."

"We mean you no harm." Peo said as his hand clasped on the handle of the dagger.

"Well, we mean you harm." The sucker yelled as he jumped at Peo and two of the other suckers lunged at Bjorn. Quick as a flash, Bjorn swung the mace and hit the dreg on the neck with a powerful strike. The other thug pulled a knife and tried to lash out at Bjorn, but the Militibus was too quick for him and with his long legs, he kicked him into the stomach and knocked him backwards. Bjorn battled with the mace against the punk with the switchblade. They were unequally matched, with the Militibus Viking taller, stronger and more skilful a fighter than the dreg he was battling against.

He turned around quickly and kicked the blade from his hand and with his sword he swung around, and the broad blade connected with the vampire's neck. With his left leg, Bjorn kicked him in the groin and the sucker fell to his knees. Swiftly, he severed the head. He didn't have time to kick the head next to the body as the other hood was lunging at him with a hunting knife in his hand.

Bjorn deftly swung the mace and the sword together and with a quick movement he crossed both hands and the street vampire lost his battle with Bjorn. Swiftly and silently, he kicked the two heads together back to the torsos and the suckers were reduced to a pile of dirt.

He looked over at his friend and ran over and helped Peo, finish off the other punks and in a flash, there were two more heaps of soot on the ground at their feet.

Both Militibus glanced around and saw that they were alone. "I thought that we got all of the lair?" Peo questioned as they ran down the alley and across to where they had parked their panigales. Without waiting for any reply, the two Militibus drove at speed out of skid row and back to Peo's place.

*****

Sister Angelica had made a ham sandwich for the young woman who was holding the doll in her arms, the woman's eyes were downcast as she lovingly stroked the cheek of the doll. Sister Angelica had smiled warmly at the woman as she led her over to the table. She sat her down and then went back over and filled a cup with hot steaming coffee and brought it over to the young woman. She patted her on the arm as she spoke to her.

Father O'Hara didn't hear what their conversation was about, but he observed his young nun's demeanour, he could see that she had won the trust of the woman, which was difficult, at the best of times. The people of the street didn't trust too easily, they had been disappointed all too often. He noticed that Sister Angelica touched the doll gently as though she were touching a newborn. The tenderness of the scene made him feel even more ashamed of why he was at the kitchen. He hung his head in shame momentarily. How could he suspect that this committed young nun was any less devoted to her role in the convent than she had been before the Militibus vampire came along? Perhaps it was only the vampire who was infatuated because she was good and he was...What was he anyway, good, evil? Tom hadn't made up his mind about that yet. As he looked over at Sister Angelica, he knew that the young nun did not encourage a liaison with the handsome blond man.

Father O'Hara felt a knot in his chest as he walked over to the table where three men were sitting drinking hot cups of coffee and playing cards.

He smiled at them as he approached the table but then a swirling white light seemed to engulf him and a suffocating grip on his heart knocked him hard and he fell to the ground holding his chest.

He could hear muffled sounds, but he couldn't understand what they were. He closed his eyes, he needed to rest. He needed sleep, oh how he needed a peaceful sleep. *Please let me sleep!* He tried to say but no words came, just the overwhelming pain in his chest.

Chapter 23

Lanny was lying on his back, and his eyes were closed as he felt the tongue of the woman caress his bare chest. She was moving on him, in a way that excited him and drove him to the brink of distraction. He needed this distraction. He needed the release she was giving him. He was hard and he wanted more of what he was getting at that moment.

Her body moved against his cock as her tongue bounded on his taut hard abs in arabesque circles. She was good, as she moved lower on him. His arms were spread out across the super king size bed, and he was close to exploding with pleasure.

A vision of the nun flashed before him as the girl who was astride him, giving him oral pleasure. Lanny wondered what it would be like to have sex with the nun!

Lanny opened his eyes quickly as the doorbell rang. He turned his head in the direction of the bedroom door. It sounded again.

"Get dressed." He growled as he pushed the woman off him and reached for his pants and hurriedly put them on and walked in a few strides out into the hallway of his luxurious apartment. He was irritated by the interruption. The mood was broken.

The doorbell sounded again, and he walked over to it and opened it. Standing outside was the nun. Tears streamed down her beautiful face. She was crying uncontrollably.

"What is it?" Lanny asked concerned as he gently led the nun into his lounge. "What's the matter, Sister?" But the nun was too distraught to speak. She just broke down and cried again.

Lanny put his arms around her and held her close to him as he listened to her heart while her body shook violently with sobs. She felt good in his arms. Too good.

The touch of her soft hands as she rested them on his bare chest, was like an electric shock to him as she cried unbearably in his arms. He could feel his own heart beating erratically as she touched his skin. The smell of her hair, hung in his nostrils. "What's happened, Sister?" He forced himself to speak, but also fearing that she may have been attacked by suckers.

"I'm...I'm..." She broke off and was too consumed with grief to continue. Lanny led her over to the sofa and sat her down. He heard the escort come into the lounge. She was fully clothed now. This disturbance from her irritated him further. He stood up and picked up his wallet and took out several hundred dollars and handed it to the woman and almost pushed her out the door. He didn't want her breathing in the same air as the nun, his sexual companion felt corrupt next to Sister Angelica.

He walked back into the lounge and went over to the drinks cabinet and poured two glasses of brandy and walked back over to the sofa and handed one to the nun. Nervously she took it from him as she looked at him.

"I've interrupted your evening." She said through her tears. "I'm so sorry but I didn't know where to go." Her voice was full of uncertainty as Lanny smiled at her and shook his head.

"You haven't disrupted anything." He said and looked into her eyes. "Why are you so upset?" He saw the tears run down her beautiful face. It pained him to see her so upset.

"It's Father O'Hara," she whispered, her voice barely audible, as she lifted the glass to her mouth. She made a face as she took a sip. This amused him. She was unused to alcohol.

"What about, the padre?" Lanny coaxed her gently.

"He was at the soup kitchen, tonight." She struggled as her chest heaved with the weight of the emotion that she was under. "He fell to the floor... he had a heart attack." She began to cry uncontrollably again.

Lanny put his arm around her shoulder and pulled her close to him and he breathed in the lavender perfume of her hair as he held her. "Is he...dead?" Lanny asked, trying to sound sensitive, he closed his eyes as his lips brushed her temple, her skin was warm and soft, so wonderfully soft. He couldn't help feeling the way that he was. But he had to remain comforting to her, she needed that and from the emotional state the young woman was in, he felt that the priest had died.

"No...I don't think so...I hope not... but" her body shook again as he pulled her closer to him. "Lanny, he is gravely ill." Sister Angelica looked up into his eyes and he could see how much she adored the priest. He could feel the pain that her heart was going through as she grieved for the inevitable. Lanny wanted to help her.

"How did it happen?" Lanny asked gently, looking deep into her eyes, and as he looked at her mouth, her lips red, soft and inviting, he wanted to kiss her. "Was he in ill health, Adeline?" He couldn't call her by her nun's name. Lanny would never call her by that name again, not given the way that he was thinking...fantasising about her. Wanting her as he did. He couldn't help it.

"I don't think he was...Oh Lanny," She rested her head on his shoulder, and he kissed the top of her head as her arm went to his shoulder. "He can't die...he's a good man." She said in utter desperation.

"What hospital is he in?" He asked and she looked up at him and for a moment, he felt that she wanted him to kiss her. He wanted to kiss her badly, to hold her close in his arms. He had to move away from her, her closeness was driving him crazy. "I'll call the Praetorian, to go see what he can find out." He stood up. He didn't trust himself not to kiss her or to touch her.

He went over to the mantlepiece and picked up his phone and called Peo. A few seconds later he heard him say hello. "Peo, it appears the padre has had a heart attack, he is in hospital." There was a long pause.

"Is he alive?" Peo asked.

"I don't know." Lanny replied. "The nun is here, but she is in a distraught state. Can you go find out?"

"Of course, Jarl." Peo replied. "I'll call over when I have news."

"Thank you, Peo." He hung up and walked back over to the sofa where the nun was sitting with her two hands clutching the glass of brandy.

"The Praetorian will call over here when he knows more." Lanny said as he sat down next to her.

"Who's the Praetorian?" She asked confused, Lanny smiled at her fondly, she was arousing sexual feelings in him again.

"My friend, Peo." He said casually.

"Isn't a Praetorian a roman soldier?" Sister Angelica asked slightly confused, but she didn't understand as she glanced at him.

"Yes, I can see that you are tired, and you've had a shock." Lanny said gently and stood up and held out his hand to her, nervously she took it. "The guest room is always made up and I can give you a shirt to sleep in. You need to sleep, Adeline." But as she was about to object, he raised his hand to stop her and smiled tenderly at her. "I will wake you as soon as Peo has news. Now come, you need to sleep." He ordered and she didn't protest as she held his hand, and he led her down the hall to the guest room.

Lanny turned on the light and went over to the bed and turned down the blankets and then went over to the dresser and opened the drawer. He took out a silk pyjamas shirt and turned and handed it to her. "There are fresh towels, and the bathroom is over there, rest now Adeline." He walked over to the bedroom door.

"Lanny," he turned to look at her, he couldn't take his eyes off her. "Thank you." He smiled at her and left the bedroom. He knew that he couldn't stay in the same room as her. He didn't trust himself not to seduce her.

*****

The doorbell buzzed and Lanny got up and walked down the hall and opened it. Peo was standing outside. He looked a little worse for the wear. "You look like you've been in battle." Lanny teased as he led him into the lounge. "Want a drink?" Peo said yes. "What's the news on the padre?" He poured two glasses of brandy and held one out to Peo.

"The priest had a stress related incident." Peo informed him and took a sip. "He should be out of hospital in a few days." Lanny motioned him to sit down.

"So, it wasn't a heart attack?" Peo shook his head. "Adeline will be happy." He said absentmindedly.

"Adeline?" Peo questioned as he looked at him.

"Sister Angelica." Lanny corrected himself quickly but swore to himself.

"Lanny, you haven't...?" Peo questioned immediately.

"Haven't what, Praetorian, made love to her?" Lanny asked a little heatedly but to the point. He gave a half laugh when he saw the look on his friend's face. "No, Peo, I haven't but I can't say that I didn't want to, but as she is a woman of faith..." He took a sip from his glass. "What caused the padre to collapse like that?" He changed the subject quickly.

"Well, earlier, Bjorn and I encountered suckers." Peo declared and Lanny stared at him. "We fought them, but we were caught by surprise." He took a sip. "Perhaps the priest has had an encounter with some too, at the hotel."

"I thought we killed the suckers." Lanny pondered to himself and stared into the gas fire. "Have more come into the city?" He asked abstractedly.

"Perhaps, the silent partner has invited more here." Peo answered and rested the glass on the edge of the armchair. "That's why I don't think you should meet them alone, Jarl."

"It's the investors, Praetorian, they won't risk bringing suckers into a public area like that bar." Lanny said confidently.

"But Jarl-"

"Save the advice, Peo." Lanny cut him off but grinned at him. "You can worry when we do battle with the suckers." He looked up and saw Adeline standing in the doorway. She looked ashen. Anxious.

"Sister Angelica," Peo called out as he stood up. "I've come from the hospital, and Father O'Hara will be fine, it wasn't a heart attack." He smiled gently at her, but she didn't return his smile. She looked concerned.

"What are suckers? And who are you going to battle?" She asked determinedly as she stood still in the doorway. Peo glanced awkwardly at Lanny who had just stood up.

"Adeline, come sit down." He held out his hand to her, but she wouldn't move. She remained frozen where she stood.

"Tell me." She demanded in an aroused voice.

"We play a tournament, a video game." Lanny was inspired and smiled warmly at her. "Peo and I are battling players we call suckers on Saturday." He looked over at Peo to back up his story.

"That's right, if we win, we get five thousand dollars." They both smiled at her. "Makes you wonder who the suckers are in this case." He half laughed and glanced away from her.

She walked over to the armchair and sat down where Lanny had sat a few minutes earlier. She seemed to have believed them. "Father O'Hara is going to be, OK?" She asked after a moment, but her voice was shaky.

"The doctor wants to keep him under observation for a few days." Peo went on and then handed the glass to Lanny. "I'll call you tomorrow, Jarl, good night." As he reached the door he turned to the nun as she sat on the armchair. "Good night, Sister." He gave Lanny a warning look, but all Lanny could see was Adeline wearing his shirt and her long shapely legs as she sat on the armchair. The desire that he had felt earlier when she first came to his apartment, had returned and he knew he couldn't remain around her.

Chapter 24

The bar was sparsely filled with various businessmen discussing issues and making deals over drinks. Lanny walked into the hotel bar and scanned the place, he saw John Josess sitting with two other men, one he knew, Frank Rostern. The other man, he assumed was the silent investor, he had his back so Lanny couldn't see his face. Lanny grinned at this.

He stood up straight and observed the scene before him for a moment. The three vultures were deep in discussion, deep in conspiring how to rip off the priest, or whoever else they crossed paths with. They didn't see Lanny at first. Then John Josess looked up when he saw Lanny walking toward him. He stood up as Lanny approached their table, and he smiled convincingly at him.

"Mr Lancnut, glad you could make it." Josess held out his hand to Lanny and they shook hands. "Frank, you remember Mr Lancnut?" Frank Rostern stood up and shook Lanny's hand. Then John Josess cleared his throat and introduced Lanny to the silent investor.

He held out his hand and the older man barely touched his hand. "Good evening." Lanny said as a slow smile spread across his face when he recognised the silent partner. He was angry with himself. He should have realised the connection immediately when they began the investigation. But he had missed it completely.

A waiter passed their table and John stopped him. "What would you like to drink, Mr Lancnut?" Lanny turned to the waiter.

"A Midleton whiskey." Lanny ordered as he sat down across from the three men. He had a view of the door and the window from this vantage point. He could also observe the Militibus concealed in the SUV parked across the road from the bar.

"Josess, says you are interested in joining our consortium." Rostern said in a gruff tone. Lanny could see the sides of his mouth turned up in a sneer, this expression was something that he had come to expect from Rostern since their previous meeting.

"If the terms and conditions meet my expectation." Lanny agreed as he looked at Rostern. "That's why I am here after all." He added and then glanced at the silent investor, he sensed a familiarity, not just a connection with this group, but something else. He was quiet and his head was bent slightly so Lanny couldn't see his eyes, but he could hear the steady beat of his heart. It was unusual.

"What are your terms, Lancnut?" Rostern asked abruptly as the waiter put the glass of whiskey on the table in front of Lanny. Lanny looked Rostern in the eyes and smirked. He would enjoy this, this game of wits. Theirs against his, but he knew he would win, they wouldn't outsmart him easily.

"Isn't that why you invited me here, to discuss your project and convince me to part with several million dollars?" He lifted the glass and said in a toasting gesture. "Tuum bonum salutem iudices." The silent investor glared but Lanny just smiled at him. He had just sussed him. Lanny knew what he was!

"Mr Lancnut is from Denmark." John Josess said happily with his perceived knowledge of the Jarl as he took a sip from his own glass. This made Lanny smile even wider. He knew that Josess was an idiot, but he just confirmed it with his ignorance.

"Well, I won't beat about the bush," Frank Rostern said gruffly. "You stand to become a very rich man if you join our conglomerate, Lancnut."

"I'm already a wealthy man," Lanny corrected without taking his eyes off the silent investor. He knew that the man was aware of who and what Lanny was. In a perverse way, this satisfied Lanny even more. It made the game a little more interesting.

"I mean seriously wealthy, boy." Rostern said eagerly. "Wealthier even than your daddy." This made Lanny smile even more as he turned to the planner.

"My father is an aristocrat, what makes you think I could be wealthier than him?" Lanny was playing him, and he could see Rostern was becoming more uncomfortable by the moment, this suited Lanny.

"Alright then, I'll ask you straight out, Lancnut," Rostern growled.

"Frank," The silent investor said in a low but arrogant voice. "Do you really want to get into bed with a bloodsucker?" This made Lanny chuckle even more as he looked across at him. He could see the venom in his expression.

"I'm sure you already have...Mr...?" Lanny asked him as he looked him flush in the face. He saw now what he was too.

"My name is unimportant." The investor snapped. "I just wonder what these two imbeciles are thinking inviting someone like you into our enterprise." Lanny laughed loudly and both Rostern and Josess looked at each other and then at Lanny. Confusion was written all over their faces. He wondered if they were aware of the men, they were about to do business with, or what and who they were? Perhaps with their greed, they just didn't care either way.

"We're all bloodsuckers here," Lanny chimed with a deep baritone voice. "Now, what I want to know is what do I get out of it? Do you want to do business, or do you just want to trade insults with me all evening, old man?" Lanny wore a serious expression as he stared at him. "I want in, and I am prepared to invest a lot more than any of you have so make me an offer and make it good or I walk." He sounded very convincing now. They all looked at him and he saw a snide smile cross the silent investor's greedy face as he held out his hand to Lanny.

"In that case, welcome aboard the Cyclades luxurious condominiums." Lanny shook hands with him, it was cold, stone cold, and he turned to the other two.

"We have a little problem here, I understood when I donated to the priest's charity, it was being used for the homeless of tent city." Lanny stoked it and reached for the glass of whiskey. The three men just laughed and shook their heads.

"Silly old fool," Rostern said. "We have a plan in motion to evict them." Lanny smiled slowly too as he watched Rostern closely.

"How do you plan on doing that?" He probed. "I assumed that they were already installed there?"

"Some of your brethren are working on it as we speak." The silent investor said and chuckled almost to himself as his entire body shook. "As for O'Hara, I have it arranged for when he comes out of hospital, he will be forced to take a position in Haiti." Lanny joined in with them and laughed as he eyed the three men.

"I'm glad to hear it." He said seriously. "So, when do you expect to begin work on the condos?" Josess tittered and Lanny glanced at him cynically.

"As soon as you sign the cheque." He spoke in an arrogant tone. "The residents will be gone in a week, but they don't matter anyway." They raised their glasses and toasted to the deal that they had just sealed.

"Which one of you bloodsuckers own the building?" Lanny asked jovially as he downed the Midleton whiskey. There was an uproar of laughter from the three of them.

"I do," the investor said smirking. "It's not the only one either. Play your cards right and there will be more Cyclades investments."

"Indeed." Lanny said and stood up. "Gentlemen, this has been a revelation." The three men roared with laughter once more, they were intoxicated with the thoughts of making more money.

"Revelation." Josess said holding his tie as he heaved with laughter. "That's a good one, for the bishop there." The silent investor shot him a warning look.

"Good evening." Lanny nodded at them and then he strolled away.

"Do you think we can trust him?" He heard Rostern ask.

"He is a vampire, he's thirsty for money." The investor said and Lanny grinned as he left the building.

Chapter 25

Luca sat back in his leather chair. He was enjoying a quiet moment. The Militibus had told him about the priest and the stress event he had had. Luca worried that the old man was in danger of dying. So far, he had been the one to hold the project together. This could kill him, or maybe, just maybe, it could be the ignition for the fire to survive.

Lanny had told him about some disturbing news regarding the plans for the hotel and the timeframe involved. It certainly wasn't good news for the residents. Or the priest.

Luca wondered if they had enough time to execute the plan that Lanny had put in place. He trusted the Jarl's judgement, as he was a skilled tactician. No, what concerned Luca was the ill health that had befallen the priest and the short time frame. It would have to run smoothly. But experience told Luca it rarely did.

Oh, what he wouldn't give for a relaxing evening with good music and fine wine! The company of a lady would be welcome too, he smiled to himself. Neither was possible until this case was over and then, Luca had promised himself some relaxation time, just for him. Surely, he was entitled to that.

The phone on his desk rang and he leaned forward and picked it up. "Hello?" He answered in a deep voice.

"Mr Meridian, I'm not disturbing you, am I?" It was Father O'Hara. He sounded chirpier than he had the last time they spoke.

"Not at all, Father." Luca answered. "Please, call me Luca."

"Thank you for your concern," Father O'Hara said in a serious tone. "Can you come see me, I have something which needs to be discussed with you."

"Of course." Luca agreed. "I'll be right over." He hung up and smoothed his hair, which had been perfectly smooth anyway. But it was habit.

Luca stood up and walked over to the coat rack and put on his long black trench coat.

Luca walked purposefully along the corridor in the hospital. He could smell death coming from some of the wards and he knew that the life blood was slowly draining from the patient inside. The smell was everywhere, so too was the smell of blood. Fresh blood! He slowed for a moment and closed his eyes briefly.

He stopped outside the door and looked both ways and entered the room. He glanced around quickly, looking for the priest.

There were six beds lined up across from each other and there were cheerful yellow curtains that separated the patients and gave privacy to them during consultation with the doctors.

Luca found the priest sitting up in the single metal bed, reading a hardback book. He looked up as Luca approached him and smiled. "Ah, Luca, thank you for coming." Father O'Hara said jovially. Luca wondered at how content he seemed considering where he was and what he had just been through. He always seemed to have a book in his hand too, Luca noted.

"How are you, Father?" Luca asked in a friendly manner as he removed his coat and placed it onto the back of the old wooden chair.

"Considering all the fuss I caused, I am fine." The older man smiled and motioned for Luca to sit down. "You came alone?" He queried as he appeared to search for someone else behind him.

"Did you want to meet with the others also?" Luca questioned him and took out his phone to call the Militibus.

"No, no, I just assumed you and the other...man went everywhere together." Luca could tell that the priest had a trust issue with Lanny, with all of them, considering his beliefs were in contravention with what the Militibus were. "Luca, I understand that Sister Angelica, spent...spent the night with Mr Lancnut." The weight of the concern balanced considerably on his shoulders.

"Yes, she did." Luca confirmed, as he leaned forward and studied the priest carefully. It was the clergyman's worst fear.

"It is inappropriate for a nun to spend the night with a man." Father O'Hara spoke but then was suddenly consumed in a fit of coughing. Luca stood up and poured the older man a glass of water and handed it to him. "Thank you." He said and handed the glass back to Luca who placed it back on the side table.

"Father O'Hara, look whatever misgivings you have toward Lanny," Luca said as he sat down on the bed. "I assure you, the Jarl acted with complete integrity. The sister's virtue was never compromised." Luca knew Lanny would never take advantage of a situation as had been presented to him that night. He was sure of it.

"You have no worries concerning his interest in Sister Angelica?" Father O'Hara voiced his concern in a serious tone. He searched Luca's face for answers.

"The Jarl's interest in the nun is purely related to the case he is working on." Luca reassured. "I can guarantee you of that." The priest nodded but he wasn't convinced and then he glanced carefully back at Luca.

"Why do you refer to him as 'the Jarl'?" Luca could see he had aroused the priest's curiosity now. He smiled at him for a moment.

"Lanny is the son of a Viking lord." Luca told him with a grin. "He also has a wicked sense of humour along with being an effete snob, but once you know him, he is loyal to the end." He glanced around the ward. "I trust him with my life."

"And you Luca, what is your background?" Father O'Hara asked in a low tone. Luca turned to look at the man sitting up in the bed. It seemed natural to tell this holy man everything about the Militibus, they had shaken him by their existence, and it was only right that he knew who the were...Once!

"I was a centurion general in the army of Rome, under Emperor Titus." Luca said proudly, then without warning a moment from his past flashed before his eyes, the moment of the eruption. He closed his eyes and then turned back to the priest. "Do you want to know about Peo and Bjorn?" He asked and the priest nodded. "Peo was a praetorian assigned to the army to the south and Bjorn, he was a berserker, fighting alongside the Viking, Leif Ericsson in Greenland. So, you see, Father O'Hara, we are not just vampires bursting with a blood lust, we are the elite, and the Militibus have honour and we live by a code." Tom O'Hara sat up straight and looked at him but then hung his head. "A code that if we break it, has serious consequences for us with our superiors back in the Sixth."

"I am ashamed of myself for lumbering you with the label of murderers." The priest said regretfully. "But I am not blind either, Luca, I can see how Sister Angelica is in awe of your Jarl, he is a handsome looking man, a man of the world, and she has never been around someone like him before." They looked at each other with the priest beseeching Luca to understand his anxiety over the Jarl's behaviour toward the nun. "But my concern is that my bishop has threatened to have her removed from the parish and if he does, it will break her heart." Father O'Hara said quietly and then took a deep breath. "It would break mine too, I am fond of her you see, she is a virtuous person." Luca watched him carefully. He could tell, from what Demis described of the priest's soul, that he too was a good man. A worthy man with faultless morals.

"We won't let that happen, Father." Luca reassured the clergyman. "When do you get to go home?"

"Tomorrow afternoon." He answered and Luca noticed that his hand had a tremor as he lifted his book off his lap. The cleric was ill, and it showed.

"Shall I collect you and take you back to your home?" Luca offered and the padre smiled warmly at him. His appreciation was evident.

"I couldn't ask that of you, Luca." He spoke timidly. "I'll take the bus." Luca laughed heartily and stood up.

"No, I will be here tomorrow after lunch." Luca said in a forceful voice. "Enjoy your book, padre." He walked to the end of the bed and turned to him and added. "The Jarl is well versed in theology if you ever need a good sparring partner." Luca laughed and walked out of the ward and left the hospital.

Chapter 26

Bjorn was strumming on his guitar in his apartment. He loved this time alone when it was just him and his collection of vinyl records where he could play the music he liked, which was gothic rock. Music that if it were played in either of the clubs, he owned, it would have the punters scattering for their lives.

He smiled as he thought of the expression on Lanny's face when he threw on a cd in his car when they drove to Vegas, he was appalled by the lyrics and the 'noise', as he referred to it. But to Bjorn, it was sheer music mastery and he loved it. So, when he learned to play the guitar, naturally it was what he played. He liked to jam with some guitarists and just hang out and debate who was or is the better guitarist and who plays better live or in a studio.

When he was growing up in the settlement of Kiruna, he played a string instrument resembling a guitar. He played it at his friend, Hardra's wedding just before they left to go to Francia on their first raid outside of their territory. They were sailing to Francia when a storm blew them off course, and for several weeks all they had done was remain at the mercy of the wind, and then they drifted further west and landed in Greenland. It had surprised the berserker warriors what they had seen. Along the coastline, the shore, was rocky and green, and it resembled nothing of what awaited them when they ventured inland, where they found ice capped mountains, it was just like Kiruna in many ways only there were not many settlements. At first, they thought it was uninhabited, but they were wrong. It had been inhabited and by people almost as fierce as the Vikings themselves.

Bjorn closed his eyes to the memory of the night that he was turned. He had been carving a piece of wood with the knife he had been given by his father. It had been cold, and he had worn an extra bearskin to keep warm. He could still feel the cold as if it were yesterday.

His mind had been full of the memories of the woman who had given him his first sexual encounter, a good luck romp before he set sail for Francia.

He hadn't heard the breaking of the sticks as he remembered the way the woman had ridden him like a horse. But he felt it, felt the unbelievable ecstasy of the feeling that enveloped him as the blood from his neck trickled out, and then he felt the pleasure as the artery was pierced and the incredible pain it gave. Oh, how he had enjoyed the pain. It had been better than the sex he had had with the village woman. The agony from the pierced artery filled him with an orgasm so powerful, he felt he would never be whole again until he felt that burn once more.

Bjorn had closed his eyes as the fangs went deeper into his neck and all reason left his mind and body. It was later that he had discovered that the sensation he felt, was his physical body slowly dying. It had taken three days for it to happen. Three long agony filled torturous days, as his mortal body, filled with venomous blood from the alpha vampire, slowly died in an excruciating death. While his new vampiric life was born, and his immortality took over, along with the awful, fiendish thirst and desire to feed on fresh mortal blood.

Bjorn closed his eyes once more as he recalled the way Leif and his clan had reacted to him. Their behaviour, after they found the lifeless body of Hardra, drained of his life's blood. A court was held, and Bjorn was blamed for killing Hardra.

No one believed him, but as the evidence against him pointed to what he had done to Hardra, along with the blood lust that coursed through him, it was worse than the beating and the banishment.

Bjorn had accepted his fate as a monster. For that was what he had become. A blood fiend. A vampire. Though at the time, he didn't know it.

Bjorn stood up and put the guitar down on the sofa. He walked over to the window and glanced out at the vista of LA. The city of angels, as it was referred to. This made Bjorn laugh, as far as the misnomer was concerned there were no angels in LA just every kind of dreg that had been refused entry to hell, and the dimensions beyond.

This city had it all, but it didn't have any angels, non that Bjorn could see, just selfish, greedy murderous dregs that tried to outsmart each other as they scuttled for a piece of the leftovers that had been thrown out in the garbage.

This was LA, this was his home, and he loved it.

Chapter 27

True to his word, Luca had called to the hospital to collect Father O'Hara and take him back to the parochial house to convalesce in the comfort of his home.

Luca helped the old man into the passenger seat of the SUV and closed the door for him and then went around to the driver's side and got in. He looked across at the man sitting beside him. He looked a lot healthier than the previous day when Luca had seen him in the hospital. He also appeared more upbeat. But his hands still tremored. This concerned Luca, he had seen people, younger than this cleric, give in to their old age and their afflictions, it signalled the decline in their mortality.

"Have there been any more developments since I spoke with you and your officers?" Father O'Hara asked plaintively as he put on his seatbelt. Luca drove out of the hospital parking lot and when he was stopped at the traffic light he turned to the priest and said gravely.

"Yes, quite a lot actually." He didn't want to worry the man, given he was poorly, but yet, he knew that he had a right to know what was going on.

"Oh, you discovered who is trying to prevent the residents from moving in." Father O'Hara asked hopefully as Luca made a right turn.

"Yes, the Jarl has been working closely on it," Luca said and glanced at him, he didn't believe it was a good idea to tell him everything. "It's better for you, Father if you don't know." He heard the priest try to contain a cough.

"Is it someone I know?" He persevered gravely. "Someone I trust?" There was a pained expression on his face at the knowledge that someone he knew and trusted was betraying him and the parish. His keen sense seemed to have kicked in, despite Luca trying to protect him from the awful truth.

"I can't say for certain, as Lanny didn't reveal the names." Luca admitted. "But Father, rest assured that my men are the best, they will stop what is harassing your residents." The priest nodded but Luca sensed his anguish once more. He could smell his despair. Nothing that Luca could say would have any effect in consoling him now.

"These people have had to struggle their entire lives," the priest said with a despairing tone. "They put their faith in me, I don't want to let them down."

"You won't let them down." Luca asserted, trying to sound as if he believed it himself, that the Militibus could stop the evictions from the hotel. He too was losing faith in the successful closure of this case.

Luca pulled up outside the parochial house and switched off the engine. As he opened the door of the car, he saw the young nun race down the steps and over to the car.

"Father O'Hara, welcome home." She almost sang with delight and Luca smiled as he saw the expression on the older man's face as he enjoyed the fuss that was being made of him. Luca could see the relief on the young woman's face too.

"You are in good hands now, Father." Luca assured him with a grin. "I'll be in touch. Good day Sister." He looked at her and for a moment he saw her sneak a glance into the car, Luca knew that she was looking for Lanny.

Luca drove back to his office and when he arrived his secretary told him that there was someone to see him.

He opened the door into his office and smiled when he saw Demis. "I didn't think you'd ever come back." Demis said grumpily from where he sat in the antique leather armchair.

"Hello Demis, I had an errand to run in town." Luca replied as he held out his hand to the old philosopher. "What brings you dimension side?"

"I would expect that retort from the Viking not from you General." He said tetchily as he sat down on the chair again. He was flustered and in a bad mood.

"Forgive me, Demis," Luca said with a repressed smile. "It was unworthy. Now what brings you here?" He walked over to the cabinet and poured two whiskies and handed a glass to Demis, who took the tumbler from him without a reply.

"How is the old priest?" Demis asked as he took a gulp of whiskey and then looked with a harsh expression at Luca.

"As well as can be expected." Luca replied and sat down.

"I hear the Jarl is seducing the nun, is that right?" Demis asked and glared at Luca.

"No, Demis, he isn't." He couldn't tell the philosopher that what Lanny was doing was light flirtation, Jarl style, as it would send Demis mad with rage. Likely to end up with Lanny being disciplined back in the Sixth, yet again.

"Really?" He asked disbelievingly. "There's a first for the Jarl. Remember the Schumann woman? The scandal that caused...hmmm."

"I'm sure he learnt from that." Luca defended as he felt the betrayal of his friend by discussing his private life with Demis.

"Another thing, he doesn't have a private life." Demis grumbled and took a sip from the glass. Luca had forgotten that the old intellectual could read minds. "You are Militibus, you are held in the highest esteem. Remember that." He scoffed. "You need to reign in the Jarl with his amorous tendencies. Shocking, they are." Demis tutted loudly.

"Of course." Luca said humouring him. They all had romantic encounters with mortal females in this dimension, it was their own private affair, he thought to himself, nothing to concern the council of Elders, or Demis for that matter. "You have news for us, Demis?" He encouraged gently, getting off the subject of Lanny's sex life.

"The influx of suckers into the city, do you know where it has come from?" Demis asked taking another sip.

"No, the leader refused to give up the source." Luca answered rapidly as he looked at the tempus viator philosophum.

"Ask him again, this time don't let him go until he reveals who it is." Luca smiled at him. He was about to make Demis angry.

"That would prove difficult, Demis." Luca said with a lobsided grin. "Lanny sent him to Gehenna."

"Of course, he did." Demis mumbled sarcastically. "Doesn't he believe in conversing first?"

"With due respect, Demis, Lanny is one of the best Militibus there is." Luca said praising his comrade, his second in command.

"Of course, he is, Lucian but he could have gotten a name, before he became axe happy." Demis amused all of them by the way he spoke. Nothing pleased him and everything bored him. "Perhaps a little less encouragement in brandishing his weapons, and more in the way of conversation, might be in order, Lucian." Demis accused vehemently.

"The Jarl has found the saboteur, and he knows who has called for the vampires to terrorise the occupants of the hostel." Luca said in a serious tone, he loved to let the philosopher rant and then take him by surprise with details of the plan they always put in play. He knew it was petty, but it was a habit he had picked up from Lanny, and Luca enjoyed it. Enjoyed it even more when Demis squirmed at the progress that they made.

"Why didn't you say so, Lucian?" Demis ranted aloud. "Who is it? Has he stopped them yet?" He asked in an aroused tone. "Has he sent them to the Tenth also?"

"He hasn't revealed it to us," Luca said sitting back in his chair once more as he studied Demis closely. "Lanny has decided to draw him out a bit more before striking." Demis shook his head, and he was getting furious again. "He knows what he is doing, Demis, he's been a tactician a long time."

"He'll get himself killed with his outlandish schemes one of these days." Demis muttered and stood up. "I'll be back in a week or so, let's hope the snob has the job done then." He muttered something as he walked to the door, but Luca didn't understand what he had said as he left.

When Demis was gone, Luca laughed loudly and finished his drink. The old coot was difficult at best and sometimes, like now, he brought out the worst in them. All of them, but particularly in the Jarl, who was known to argue with him, which inevitably proved futile. But he did it just to prove a point with the old boy.

Chapter 27

Lanny was sitting at the piano in his penthouse, he was playing a piece which Clara had written, she had said it was for him, but he knew it was for her husband, Robert. He had loved that about her, she flirted outrageously and then made men feel persecuted because she had caused the situation to begin with and then accused them of it. He smiled, oh how he had enjoyed her company, her wit, and her body.

He closed his eyes as he played the piece, each note as melodic and perfect as she had known it would be. Her artistic precision evident in every note. Her genius ever present in her compositions.

The doorbell buzzed loudly, and Lanny looked over at it and reluctantly stopped playing and walked over to the door and opened it. Adeline was standing there.

"Hi," she said as she nervously looked into the hallway.

"Hello Adeline." Lanny greeted and stepped aside, to let her into the apartment. She walked hesitantly into the hall. "What brings you out so late at night?" He asked as she followed him into the lounge.

"I wanted to see you." She spoke softly and lowered her eyes. "To thank you for your kindness when Father O'Hara was taken to hospital." She added swiftly. This made him smile as he looked her up and down favourably.

"No thanks needed, Adeline." He motioned for her to sit down, and she did.

"Was that you, playing the piano?" She asked nervously. Lanny smiled at her and sat down beside her. He saw her glance at his chest, his shirt was held closed by just one button, his trousers were closed only by the zip, which wasn't fully fastened. He wore no shoes, as he was relaxing and hadn't planned on going out.

"Yes, do you like classical music?" He gazed at her tenderly, and she smiled shyly. Her mannerisms were sweet, and she gave away her emotions with them. Lanny knew that she lusted for him, though she probably didn't know what it meant. But he did, and he desired her, more than he had any woman before.

"I do, I enjoy listening to some pieces." She admitted softly. "What was the piece you were playing?"

"Clara Schumann's three romances." He told her as he studied her facial expression. "It's an exquisite piece. Don't you think?" She nodded and lowered her eyes, afraid to look at him. Her eyes giving away her yearning for him. Just as he longed for her.

"You are so cultured." She whispered and he tilted her chin so she would look at him. He saw a sadness in her eyes now, a deep sorrow which seemed to consume her. He moved closer to her, and he could feel her pulse beat fast. This excited him as he bent his head, Adeline closed her eyes in anticipation of their lips meeting, but instead Lanny just kissed her cheek softly. Her skin was soft, smooth, perfect. She excited him, she made him aware of his power, aware of what it was like to desire something so beautiful. Lanny craved her. He wanted her, wanted her body, he wanted her in bed next to him, making love to him.

Lanny smiled and stood up and walked over to the piano. "Let me play something for you, Adeline." He sat down and began to touch the keys lightly and closed his eyes as the passion that he was feeling for her consumed him. He knew that he could never take her, not like he had with Clara. That had been different, it had been raw, it had almost shattered her, with its intensity, but it had made her crave him even more. Their affair had been brief, very sexual and all consuming, for both of them.

He felt Adeline sit down next to him as he played the piano. He smelt her longing for him as she rested her hand delicately on his leg. Lanny stopped playing and looked at her wantonly. She was beautiful and for the first time, he noticed that she wore lipstick. A subtle shade of pink, it suited her. He knew that it wasn't an object that she would have in her toiletry bag, and he wondered if she had gone to the drug store and secretly purchased it to wear for him. This thought excited him, excited him to know how badly that she wanted him to kiss her.

"I...tried not..." Adeline inhaled deeply and then reached out to touch his face. It felt like a shock on his skin. "I tried to stop myself coming here." She said as her fingers touched his cheek. Lanny looked into her green eyes, and he saw the conflict within her. Conflict, which he had caused her.

"Adeline," he spoke in a low tone. "You know you shouldn't be here." He looked at her, he wanted to devour her body, to take what he coveted, to take her. "You are a woman of faith, and I am a man, forbidden to you." He looked deep into her eyes. He couldn't deny how he was feeling at that moment. What he wanted to do, and do with her.

"I don't want to be a nun anymore." She whispered as she reached for his mouth with hers and kissed him quickly. "I want you, Lanny." Her soft voice caressed the air. He felt her arms go around his neck and he bent his head and their lips met, as their kiss deepened, he parted her lips with his tongue. She felt so good, so pure. It would feel good to take from her what she offered, and what he wanted, had needed from the first moment he saw her.

"Adeline," he murmured huskily as he pulled her into his arms and kissed her passionately. Lanny could hear the blood flowing from her heart as it filled her veins. His excitement at hearing it, grew stronger. He needed to have her. The sound of her blood, and her heart beating consumed his heightened senses. He needed to ravage her body, take her right there.

His hand caressed her breast as he felt her nipple respond to his touch, Lanny could hear her sweet murmurs as she felt new feelings that she had never experienced before. Adeline responded to him. Lanny groaned as her hand covered his bulging hardness, he felt like he could explode right there with just the material of his pants separating his cock from her delicate hand. He needed to take her, he needed to make love to her...He needed...

But he knew he couldn't, he had to stop this before it got to a point where he wouldn't be able to stop. Lanny pulled away from her and stood up. He walked over to the window and glanced out of it. His arousal was very obvious. He could feel the change happening within him, he could feel his fangs move, descend, he had to stop it. His teeth were beginning to multiply, he was getting the vampire urge to feed.

This was happening so quickly, because she was so pure, it didn't take long to take hold of him.

Lanny knew that he couldn't let her see him like that. "Sister Angelica, you better leave." He snapped at her in a deep tone without turning around. She couldn't see his monstrous vampiric side, Lanny couldn't, wouldn't allow it.

"Lanny, don't you want me?" She asked confused by the sudden change in him, almost in tears. He turned around and looked at her. She was so beautiful, so innocent, so pure. "I want you to take me to bed." She had no idea what she was offering him, and she had no idea what it was doing to him. His fangs were almost fully descended now as were the mandibular canines.

"Let me call you a cab, Sister Angelica." He walked over to the phone and called a cab. Lanny was struggling now, battling to keep the vampire within him from showing the ugly side of what he was.

"Why...why don't you want me?" She cried after him. He hung up and looked at her. If only she knew just how much he wanted her and what it was doing to him.

"You are a nun, Sister." Lanny said in a harsh tone. "I don't want you sexually. Now go, please." He walked out of the lounge and held open the door for her and she looked at him and all he saw was the humiliation written in her body language, but he was powerless at that moment to tell her how he felt about her, how he really felt. That he wanted to take her to his bed, there was nothing that he would like more to happen than to make her his mate, to give her pleasure that he knew her body would give to him. But if he gave in to his carnal desire, Lanny knew what it would do to her if he did, and he couldn't bear that.

She left and he slammed the door after her, but he wanted to open it and run after her. For a moment he turned the latch on the door and opened it briefly, only for a moment but then he banged it hard again. He had to let her go.

Lanny walked into the lounge and poured a large brandy and drank it down in one gulp. He had come close to revealing his true self and he knew that Adeline, though she wasn't in grave physical danger from him, he wasn't an alpha vampire and couldn't turn her. He would have bled her, sucked her blood as he took her purity.

Adeline had lost some of her faith because of him. Lanny couldn't be alone with her again. He would have to make sure of that.

Angrily he stormed into the bedroom and removed his shirt and trousers, he threw them in a crumpled ball at the wall. He dressed in his leathers and strode back down the hall to the closet where he kept his sword and axe.

Lanny grabbed his helmet and left the penthouse in a blaze of fury.

*****

He drove like a maniac along the streets, pushing the panigale as hard as it could go. Rushing through the traffic lights as if they didn't exist. The engine roaring in response to his murderous rage.

Lanny glanced across the road, near the darkened alley and saw the two werewolves walking casually along the street and then they turned the corner. As if beckoning for him to follow, he turned the bike and followed in the direction of the dregs.

He switched off the engine and removed his helmet and placed it carelessly on the seat. A quick investigation of his surroundings showed him that the two wolves were doing more than talking to the two suckers in the alley, the wolves were dealing drugs.

Lanny removed his sword and axe from their holders and strode down the street and as he approached the four dregs, the female wolf howled and made to run away but he threw the axe and it landed between her shoulders, knocking her to the ground instantly, blood oozing down her back.

"Hey, man, what the hell?" The female's mate shouted and aggressively came toward Lanny, full of bluster. Lanny lashed out with the blade of his sword and beheaded the wolf.

He marched over to the slain female and pulled the axe from her body, but he could hear the feint whimpers as she was slowly dying. Lanny glared at her on the ground and without feeling, he plunged the sword between her ribs and finished her off.

Lanny turned to look at the two suckers, they were young, not much older than twenty. Their eyes were fixed on him, they seemed paralyzed with fear, as they didn't try to escape or to run away. *Scum!* Lanny thought to himself.

"Look we didn't mean any harm." The skin headed vampire defended. "We're sorry." He began to walk backwards as Lanny stomped over to where he stood. Without a word, the Jarl raised his blade and severed the head.

He turned around quickly when he saw the other punk begin to run, and Lanny ran after him, he reached out and grabbed him by the collar and then flung him against the wall.

"I hate your kind." Lanny shouted at him, but his rage was uncontrollable. "You are a scourge to this dimension." He stared at the youth, his fangs were beginning to hurt him, they weren't retreating and his lust for violence was burgeoning.

"Man, look we were only going to do it one time." The thug lied. Lanny shook his head and grinned at him. He could smell his fear, the youth wasn't as strong as the Viking, nor was he trained as Lanny was.

"Requiem in inferno." Lanny roared and beheaded the sucker sending him to the Tenth.

He stepped back from the light as it consumed the body and he watched it, waited for the pile of soot and then yelled and kicked the dirt pile until it had scattered and all that remained was what had blended with the soil from the side of the embankment.

Lanny sheathed his sword back in its scabbard and placed the axe back in the holder on his belt. His breathing was erratic as the adrenaline coursed through his veins like bane.

He looked around, he was alone in the darkened street. The evidence of the carnage he had caused with his Norse fury now dissipated from view. All he could see was little traces of soot.

Lanny walked quickly back to his panigale and put on his helmet, he pressed the button to start the powerful machine, and tore back the way he had come.

His rage slowly leaving him, and his vampire teeth finally receded back where they remained hidden from the world.

He had lost control of his temper, just as he had after he had been turned and he had killed his Viking friend, Dag. Lanny wasn't proud of himself then and he wasn't proud of his actions now either.

Lanny turned on the shower and stepped under the hot water, it cascaded over his long blond hair, his guilt over the events of the evening had nothing to do with the dregs, but everything to do with how he had treated Adeline.

He couldn't forgive himself for that!

Chapter 28

The four Militibus were having dinner before Lanny was to join the silent investor for their 'private', meeting.

Luca laughed heartily as Peo and Bjorn outdid each other with their juvenile jokes. They had been vulgar of course but that was how Peo was, he liked to shock everyone around him with his wit and sometimes he went a little too far with the vulgarity. This was one of those occasions where he was happy that there were no one of a sensitive disposition nearby as they would surely be offended, as had happened numerous times before.

He looked across at Lanny, he was quiet, subdued, which was unusual for him. Luca wondered if his second in command was apprehensive about the meeting, but he knew that Lanny was more than capable of defending himself, he was a strong fighter, if it came to it. He was after all, a Viking.

"Jarl, you have said little this evening." Luca remarked to him as he refilled their glasses with red wine.

"Forgive me, General," Lanny said quietly. "I am not good company." The others turned and looked at him with an incredulous look.

This wasn't like the Viking to be so withdrawn, as he was usually the life of the party. He was always great company.

"Is everything alright Lanny?" Bjorn asked, a little concerned as he looked at his comrade.

"Everything is fine, Berserker," Lanny shrugged it off and then smiled at him. "Can't I have just one, off day?" He jeered as he took a sip from his wine glass.

Luca wasn't convinced that the Jarl was OK. What Demis had said concerned him too. But he also knew Lanny and he hoped that he wouldn't be so foolish to take it further with the nun. The Jarl knew what he would risk, not just physically, but also with the council of Elders.

"How about we finish off this fine evening at my club?" Bjorn announced jovially to his friends. "Let me introduce you to some fine gothic rock." They all laughed, except for Lanny. His mood was sullen.

Peo and Bjorn stood up and so did Luca, but as he turned to look at the Jarl he said to his friends. "Give me a moment." He sat down again on the chair next to Lanny and asked. "What is wrong, Jarl?" Lanny looked blankly at him, and he could see that he was forcing a smile.

"What do you mean, General?" Lanny always used their titles when he didn't want to show his true feelings. This was one of those times.

"Are you nervous about the meeting?" Luca assumed, convinced it was something to do with his mood, he was worried, but Lanny just smiled and shook his head.

"I have raided many villages, plundered great treasures, General," he bragged as he looked at Luca. "I am a Viking, I fear nothing." Behind his great words, Luca could sense the battle he was fighting was within himself, he was transparent. But the battle this time was an internal one, with potentially terrible consequences.

"Lanny, I am your commanding officer and your friend." Luca said earnestly as he picked up the almost empty glass of wine. "You are my finest officer, and my best friend but I know bullshit when I hear it. Now, are you going to tell me what troubles you or not?" Lanny looked at him for a moment, undecided if he should confide to Luca as a friend or as his commander.

"Luca, I appreciate what you are trying to do," Lanny said in an intense tone. "But there is nothing that can be done for me, not now."

"Is it the nun?" Luca broached with him. Lanny nodded grimly. "Did you sleep with her?" He asked him outright, even though it was none of his business. A slow smile swept across the Jarl's handsome face as he looked at Luca.

"No, General, I didn't sleep with her." Lanny admitted after a minute or so. "She came to my apartment two nights ago, ready to give herself to me, we kissed passionately, and I let it go too far and felt the change beginning." He looked at Lanny.

"Have you forgotten what happened with Clara?" Luca warned. Lanny just laughed.

"With Clara it was just sex, nothing significant, General." They both looked at each other for a moment. "Adeline, was willing to give up her virtue to me and the beast within almost took it."

"But you didn't Lanny." Luca said, trying to reassure him. "I know Demis senses something is up with you." Luca informed him but Lanny just laughed at this.

"The disappointed intellectual is aware for a change." He joked and Luca could clearly see he was conflicted. "As usual, I am the source for his anxiety and his ulcer." Luca laughed briefly and hesitated as he struggled with his thoughts. "My true monstrous self, surfaced, before Adeline left, almost as if it was always there, hidden ready to show itself." Luca watched him as he paused and played with his glass. "No, she didn't see me for what I really am." Luca listened carefully to him, and he continued. "But the worst part in all of this, I went out and patrolled, I slayed some dregs like some kind of hero, ridding the streets of scum. But I'm not a hero, Luca, I am a murderous vampire, a killer, with a lust for blood that is insatiable, just as the padre said." It was clear to Luca, that the Jarl was in a crisis and needed help, and quickly.

"Can you complete the mission?" Luca asked worriedly.

"Yes, as long as I stay away from Adeline." Lanny admitted. "Once the mission is complete, the philosopher can take me to the sextam dimensionem praetorium, to be drained of my venom and then feed on selected blood suitable for, my social standing, then I shall be a good Tempus Militibus again." He flashed his brilliant smile but beneath it, and despite his bravado, he looked troubled, and Luca was concerned too. The last thing that was needed was for the Jarl to lose his way and give in to his primal vampiric instincts.

Chapter 29

Lanny wore his long leather coat, he wore no shirt, as was his preference when he fought. His leather pants clung to him, and his long blond hair sleeked back off his face and hung down his back like a silken mane. He was a gorgeous creature, and he knew it.

He walked with purpose to the hotel, where he was meeting with the silent investor. He didn't trust him, but he knew that if he turned up with his comrades, it would frighten off the investor and the meeting wouldn't take place. Lanny couldn't allow that to happen. Besides this was something that he had to do by himself.

Lanny walked over to the lift in the lobby and pressed the button. He waited but the elevator never came. It was stuck on the twelfth floor. He swore and began to walk quickly up the steps.

By the time he reached the twelfth floor, the smell assaulted his nose. He knew there were suckers in the building. He hated vampires more than he hated any of the other dregs that he sent to the Tenth.

He opened the door and walked out onto the roof and glanced around. Lanny didn't see anyone there. Then he heard the feint whimper and as he turned his head, he saw her.

Lanny strode over to where she stood. Her face was blackened with dirt and grime. Her hair was filthy and matted. Her clothes, torn, and smelled of urine. Her hands were tied behind her back and there was a dirty rag gagged in her mouth. She was terrified.

He untied her hands and removed the gag from her mouth, immediately and fearful of him, the woman backed away from him and cowered against the water tank. Lanny pitied this poor pitiful mortal.

"Who did this to you?" Lanny asked as he knelt in front of her. The woman began to whimper, then her moans became a scream. Lanny tried to sooth her, but it just made her worse. "Stay here, out of sight, I will help you. Do you understand?" She just cried loudly and all he could do was to back away from her. She was hysterical now.

"How touching." A man's voice said, and he turned around and saw the investor, he had two suckers, flanked either side of him and then Lanny noticed two others standing by the door. "I never knew vampires were so kind." He mocked and laughed at his own joke. The suckers with him, joined in the hilarity. Lanny could see their fangs were lowered and the rows of teeth had already been used to torture feed. They disgusted him.

"I am not like those thugs with you." Lanny said as he glanced at them with disdain.

"No, indeed, you are worse, you pretend to help the poor but instead you steel from them, isn't that right Mr Lancnut?" He jeered him again and began to walk over to the wall. His corruption had surfaced and distorted his features, making him even uglier than he appeared when Lanny first saw him at the bar.

"Aren't you describing yourself?" Lanny goaded as he carefully kept the bloodsuckers in his sight. He was ready to do battle if he had to.

The investor laughed loudly. "How do you like my building?" He asked changing the subject quickly as he looked

Lanny, up and down. "It will be a great addition to this desolate area, don't you think?" Lanny walked over to where he stood and glanced over the wall. Below he could just about make out some of the tents pitched along the sidewalk. During the daylight hours, as far as the eye could see, all that was visible was tent after tent. The area was a cesspit of deprivation, and no one cared. The vicinity had become synonymous with the homeless crisis in LA since the thirties. Earning it the dubious title of skid row or as he was familiar with now, tent city.

"You would rather build luxury condos instead of fulfilling your promise to those people down there?" Lanny asked and looked guardedly over at the suckers near the escape door.

"Here I was believing you were like me, Lancnut, wanting a piece of the money that these apartments will yield us." He guffawed loudly and his belly shook with his mirth. "I know that you no more feel anything for those leeches down there than I do, Lancnut, so don't pretend." He waved his hand indicating the people below them. "I have tried to help, I walked amongst them, like O'Hara does but I don't like their sense of entitlement, their ungratefulness." His features were twisted with revulsion once more at the existence of the homeless.

"But you're a man of faith, isn't it in your remit to do as the padre does and save them, give them shelter?" He snorted now and shook his head.

"You don't strike me as being naïve, Lancnut?" he said snidely. "I don't believe you have morals any more than I do." He cackled again at the very idea that anyone would want to help someone with so much hopelessness.

"I believe in right and wrong, Bishop." Lanny declared and reached his hand inside his coat and felt for the handle of the axe.

"Really, of course you don't. You seduced an innocent nun and then brag about your morality." Bishop Corkery laughed at him. "Tell me, did it feel good to take her innocence? Or perhaps she was already known to man." Lanny knew he was trying to bait him, and it wasn't working.

"You are mistaken, Bishop," Lanny jeered, while smirking at him. "The vestal is intact; she has not been known to me." The Jarl looked straight into his face and the bishop quickly turned away. "What's the matter, Corkery, can't stand to have me read your body language and know what you truly are?" He saw him raise his hand and in an instant one of the thugs lunged at Lanny, he swung the axe and it connected with the sucker's arm and knocked the knife out of his hand. With a quick movement, Lanny brought the axe down on his hand and it flew off the vampire's arm and landed at the bishop's left foot. Corkery stepped backward.

The punk yelled but Lanny drew his sword and rotated it in his right hand. He lashed out at the sucker's head, partially beheading him.

The other three hoodlums ran at him, but Lanny turned and swung around brandishing the axe at the criminal to his right as he did so. He dropped him as the axe connected with his chest. The slow kill was always the most enjoyable.

He cried out a bloodcurdling war cry as he turned and violently lashed out with the axe on the skull of the sucker. He dropped to his knees and Lanny lunged at the other monster with the bald head as he pulled the switch blade knife and tried to cut Lanny but missed.

The Jarl kicked him high in the stomach and threw the axe at him, it lodged in the sucker's skull and with his sword raised and poised Lanny launched it at his head and beheaded him, sending him to the Tenth.

He looked at the other beast and saw him back away and Lanny smiled at him and shouted. "Sanguinem in inferno requiem." His sword connected with his head, and it went flying through the air.

He walked over to where the sucker had dropped with his axe buried in his skull. Lanny pulled it out and walked away as the corpses of the vampires turned to dust.

He looked up and saw that the bishop had grabbed the homeless woman and dragged her screaming over to the wall.

"You don't have to hurt her." Lanny shouted at him and stared at the clergyman. Bishop Corkery wore an evil smile and laughed as he pushed the woman at the wall.

"But I do," he said indignantly. "For every one of them that lives, it puts my project further down the ladder." Lanny glared at him.

"That's what killing those people is about? Money?" Lanny was irritated now by the investor, but as he listened to the fear in the woman's heart, he felt sorrow for her and her predicament. "Is that all you care about?"

"Don't lecture me, vampire," Corkery said in a wild voice. "I earned this hotel. I put up with these stinking leeches while my colleagues languished in luxury over in Beverley Hills and Calabasas." He was aroused with rage again.

"That was your vow, when you became a man of the cloth." Lanny tried to reason with him, but he knew it was futile, as he walked closer to try and save the fearful woman he was holding. "You took a vow of poverty bishop." He said and stopped when he saw Corkery shake the woman, violently.

"Like you did when you became the monster you are?" Corkery hissed at him. "What little you know, vampire." Lanny stared at him horrified, the bishop was the polar opposite to the priest, with his kind gesture to help people.

"I didn't ask to be a vampire," Lanny raised his voice angrily. "I was wronged when this was done to me." Bishop Corkery howled loudly again. His eyes now reflected his maddening arousal.

"Yes, I know and oh how wonderful it was to take your life." He shouted at him. "The marauding heathens sacking my home, killing my monks. Oh, it was sweet taking your life and making you what you are." He stared at Lanny. "A vicious blood thirsty monster, who is cursed for eternity." Corkery laughed demonically.

"You?" Lanny questioned as he stared at him. "You were the alpha who turned me?" The bishop laughed manically now and shoved the woman against the wall, hatred flared in his eyes as she cried out and he picked her up and flung the poor forgotten woman over the wall, hurtling to her death.

Lanny raised his sword high and lunged at the bishop as he backed away from the Militibus officer. The Jarl weaved his axe and his sword in unison and as he connected the blade against the chest of the priest, he smiled sardonically.

"You will have a horrendous time in the Tenth, bishop." Lanny promised him in his deep baritone voice. "I would love to play with you, to torture you as you did that woman you just murdered but," he grabbed the bishop's hair and pulled his head back and scraped the blade along his throat, cutting him just below his Adam's apple. The thick dark red blood, trickling over his skin.

"Militibus don't torture, they kill quickly." Corkery goaded but Lanny just grinned. "But *your* instinct is to torture, isn't it, vampire, isn't it?" he hounded.

"You forget, bishop, I am still a Viking." Lanny yelled. "A Militibus Viking but it is heathen blood that still courses through my veins just as it is venomous blood in yours." Lanny smiled at him as his sword cut into the skin. "The other Militibus aren't here so I am free to torture you as I see fit, monk." He cut a little deeper into his skin, delighting in his game now.

"Go on, Jarl, drink it," The bishop coaxed as he smiled. "What do you care about these mortals anyway, when we could build an empire here, think of the money, the power you can have. Imagine taking by force, once more, what you want, not having to obey the Militibus code." Lanny smiled at him. "Think what I made of you before, you are a Viking, a heathen marauder, a bloodsucking vampire."

"Money and power just for us?" Lanny asked grinning. "No one to care about?"

"That's right, Jarl, drink, I give my blood, as an alpha." Lanny could see the aroused look in his face. He was beside himself in his own infallibility. "I gave my venom to you before, take my blood again and drink. Drink, you monster."

"Turn your head, monk," Lanny demanded as the bishop did what he asked and without warning, Lanny beheaded him with one swift fell of the axe. The head rolled on the ground and Lanny could see the eyes, open and wild, still mocking. Still full of hatred. Still putrid!

He stood up and picked up the head and looked at it for a moment and then threw it onto the body and stepped away.

He didn't turn as the bright light filled the rooftop and the monk who had turned him into a murderous vampire lay on the roof in a heap of soot. Lanny looked at the pile for a moment and then let out a blood curdling cry. He had just taken vengeance on the alpha for the residents of skid row. He had avenged his own murder and damnation, and his condemnation to this life of immortality, a life he never asked for but now was forced to live.

It felt good, for all of the time it took to behead the bishop and send him to the Tenth, but that was all the satisfaction Lanny got from it.

Chapter 30

Lanny stepped under the water in the shower, he rested his hands against the wall and closed his eyes. The warm clear water caressed his muscular body, giving him something to focus on. It had been a difficult night and he needed to forget what had happened. He couldn't though. He had lived with it since that faithful raid on the island of Lindisfarne.

For centuries he had vowed to kill the vampire that had turned him into the beast he tried to hide away. But he didn't know that he would ever fulfil that promise. Now that he had, it was almost an anticlimax for him. He didn't feel good like he had thought that he would, he didn't feel vindicated either. All he felt was remorse that he couldn't save the poor woman from being murdered by the alpha vampire.

He turned off the water and wrapped a towel around his waist. Lanny walked into the bedroom and put on the silk pyjamas bottoms, he picked up the shirt and sniffed the air. It was the shirt that Adeline had worn the night that she stayed in his guest room, he could smell the lavender. Lanny rolled it up and threw it on the floor. He put on the black silk robe and walked out of the bedroom and into the lounge.

He pressed play on the stereo and the beautiful strains of Clara's three romances filled the room with its exquisite notes. Lanny poured himself a large glass of vintage red wine and took a sip. It tasted good, ripe, full bodied and intense, like him. It suited his mood. He was pensive.

With the glass in his hand, he walked over to the window and glanced out. The lights of the metropolis lit up the sky. The city was alive, its heart was pulsating with life, and he could feel his own immortal heartbeat in time to the throbbing town that was now his home. Where he had made his life.

Lanny took a sip of wine, it was good, it filled the void he felt at that moment but as he smiled, he decided to call the agency and have them send over someone to alleviate the adrenaline which had built up inside him since he battled earlier. The last one they had sent was good, she had known what he wanted but she wasn't Adeline.

Chapter 31

Luca was pacing up and down in his apartment. He hadn't heard from Lanny since he had gone to meet with the silent partner. Although he didn't always check in with Luca, he was particularly worried this time because of what Lanny had revealed to him some nights earlier. About the nun, and the dregs. It wasn't good.

Sometimes, Lanny had been a hothead and he had been saved by the others when he found himself in certain situations but this time the Jarl had refused to allow the Militibus to accompany him to the meeting. It was like he was doing penance for how he felt, for his perceived crimes.

Peo believed that it was a mistake, that he had had a feeling Lanny was walking into a trap. Peo was very intuitive. Bjorn didn't feel as concerned as Peo, but he was worried that Lanny might lose his temper and leave a mess behind him. A mess that could be difficult to clean up.

Luca felt like a drink, but he didn't want to let on that he was concerned and if he had a whiskey so early, that's exactly what Lanny would think. His gift of observation was always amplified.

The doorbell buzzed and Luca walked over and opened it. He smiled, with relief when he saw the Jarl standing outside.

"Hello General." Lanny greeted as he walked into the lounge followed by Luca. He saw him look around and then the Jarl smiled and asked. "Where's your drink?" Luca laughed, but he knew what Lanny was referring to.

"Isn't it a little early, Jarl?" They both chuckled.

"Weren't you even a little concerned about me, General?" Lanny teased and Luca shook his head and grinned.

"You're a big boy, Jarl." Luca laughed. "So how did it go?" He watched with interest as Lanny walked over to the sofa and sat down, with his arms stretched out along the back of the couch.

"Peo was right." Lanny confessed as he looked at Luca. "The partner came with four suckers. It was a trap." Luca walked over to the chair opposite and sat down.

"What did you do?" He asked cautiously as he glanced at the Jarl, trying to read his body language.

"Well, they were easy to kill, what was concerning," Lanny looked at Luca in a grim way. "The partner threw the victim, a homeless woman over the wall, she plunged twelve floors." Luca shook his head, although he knew it was cruel but sometimes mortals were collateral damage.

"Poor woman." Luca said sympathetically. "Did she live at the hotel?"

"I don't believe she did." Lanny replied gravely and he looked pensive. "Perhaps she was on the waiting list, at any rate the padre will know."

"There's something you're not telling me, Jarl." Luca said as he watched Lanny closely. He knew the Viking well, and he knew when he was keeping something back, like he was now.

"You're very perceptive tonight, General." Lanny gave him a sharp smile, but he was subdued, he was burdened with something that was weighing him down.

"I know who the partner and owner of the building was," He looked at Luca. "It was the bishop we met coming out of the padre's house, the priest's boss." Luca stared sharply at him.

In the time that they had been helping those in need, very little surprised him but this did. This was not what he could have predicted at all.

"You said was. What happened?" Luca asked in a serious voice as he picked up on Lanny's tone.

"I killed him." Lanny replied in a nonchalant voice. Luca stared at him in disbelief.

"You did what?" Luca bellowed at him. "Why did you do that?"

"I had to kill him, General, he had to be sent to Gehenna." There was no emotion in the Jarl's voice as he looked him straight in the eyes. "For his crimes."

"Why, Lanny, that wasn't your mission." Luca said in a raised voice once more. This was typical of the Jarl and his hot-headed temper, reacting violently as he frequently did. He sometimes got too carried away when he fought.

"Bishop Corkery wasn't mortal," Lanny admitted expressionlessly as he looked at him. "He was a sucker, that's why he knew what we were from that first meeting, and why he could summon the vampires into the metropolis." He was detached now.

"I don't understand why you didn't just ban him to the Seventh or Eighth dimension." Luca said as he glared at his rebellious Militibus officer.

"The bishop was the alpha vampire who turned me at Lindisfarne." Lanny said unemotionally. "It was my right, as a Militibus to take revenge and show no mercy." He stood up and looked at Luca. "That is what I did, not for my murder, but for that poor woman he killed mercilessly in front of me." Luca looked intently at him. He read him. The Jarl was telling the truth. He was a good man, he tried to keep it hidden from everyone, but Lanny had honour and integrity as Luca always knew that he had.

"Let's go and inform the priest." Luca announced and walked to the door, and they left the apartment.

Chapter 32

They drove in silence to the parochial house. Lanny sat back in the seat of Luca's car. He was thinking of nothing in particular as they sped to the home of Father O'Hara. All he wanted was to get the meeting over with as quickly as possible.

Every now and then he glanced out of the window at the passing buildings. This part of the city seemed even more desolate than his first impression had been. He didn't like it. He preferred his own part of town.

Luca parked the car and switched off the engine and forced a smile as he got out. Lanny opened the door and followed his commanding officer up the steps and waited for the door to be opened. He let out a long slow sigh. It was agonising being there.

Lanny really didn't want to be there. He didn't want to see Adeline. He couldn't face her. She was his Achilles heel. She always would be. His behaviour to her when she offered him her body was nothing short of deplorable. It wasn't Adeline's fault that he was the way he was, she was blameless in everything.

The door opened and the jolly old housekeeper led them into the library where, Father O'Hara was sitting by the fire, he was reading a book. He smiled at them and motioned for them to sit down. Luca sat on the opposite armchair to the priest and Lanny, tentatively sat down on the sofa. He felt uncomfortable just being there.

"You are looking well, Father," Luca remarked in an upbeat voice, and the priest gave him a kindly grin and then he glanced across at Lanny.

"It's amazing how the body heals itself with certain relaxation." Father O'Hara said as he smiled at both of them. "I'll call for tea, or would you prefer some sherry?" He asked in a friendly tone. His manner was welcoming but Lanny wasn't in tune with it.

"Tea is fine." Luca said much to the disapproval of Lanny who shot him a look of disapproval. Luca didn't seem to care whether Lanny could use a stiff drink or not.

They exchanged some pleasantries while they waited for the tea to be brought in, but Lanny didn't say very much.

The door to the library opened and the housekeeper came in with a tray and left it down on the coffee table. She smiled at them and left.

"The nun isn't here today?" Lanny couldn't help asking. He had to know she was alright. He felt responsible for her. It was clear from the way that he evicted her from his apartment that she was...would still be upset. She wouldn't have ever been spoken to the way that Lanny yelled at her that night.

"No, Sister Angelica is helping, Sister Rose in the soup kitchen this afternoon." Father O'Hara said cautiously as he poured them tea. "She spends a lot of her time there in the afternoons now." He handed Lanny a cup and saucer, which he took from him without saying anything.

"We have good news for you Father." Luca spoke candidly as he took the cup from him. The priest looked up at him with a raised eyebrow and Luca continued. "You will have no more bother in relation to the hotel and its residents. You can continue to make the other rooms ready to receive the next homeowners." Lanny watched as the look of sheer relief swept over the priest's face. He saw the aura, that surrounded him brighten at the news.

"But how?" He asked. "How did you do it?" Luca looked at Lanny to give the priest the details.

"The owner of the building gave up his right to the hotel." Lanny said and forced himself to look at the priest. "As for the planner, well the authorities are questioning him as we speak for corruption and bribery." He didn't feel the need to tell the priest that his bishop was a bloodsucking vampire. He would spare his faith that. The Tempus Militibus had caused quite enough crisis to his devotion as it was.

"I owe you an apology, Lanny." Father O'Hara said with a timid smile. "I didn't believe you when you warned me about them. I only saw what they offered."

"They wanted it all for themselves, they saw the value in the site it stood on." Lanny said as he took a sip of tea. "Not everyone has good intentions, padre." He smiled genuinely now at the priest.

"You may remember, my bishop." Father O'Hara commented as the two Militibus stood up. "He's retired and has gone to live amongst the poorest of the poor in Haiti." He said as he accompanied them to the door. "Funny but he never struck me as the type to care about the less fortunate." Lanny smiled at him. "But doesn't that beat Banagher, as my dear father used to say when people surprised him." He nodded as he clasped his hands together.

"Sometimes people can surprise you padre." There was teasing in his voice. "Take care and I will expect you to discuss your philosophy with me sometime." Lanny grinned warmly at him. He liked the clergyman, despite his original misgivings, liked him more every time he was in conversation with him.

"It will be a pleasure to converse with you, Lanny." The priest said and he opened the door for them, and they left.

*****

Lanny parked his car and got out. He looked around and saw people scurrying with purpose as they collapsed their tents. He smiled at this; he could sense their excitement as they prepared for their new lives away from the street.

He looked once more and then walked the short distance to the soup kitchen.

Lanny stood outside for a moment, and he saw her clearing away dishes and walking into the back and then came back again to clear away more delph. She looked as beautiful as ever, even in her dark shapeless dress and her severe hairstyle. She was everything that he had ever wanted in a woman, but he could never have with her. Ever.

Lanny walked over to the door and went inside. He looked over at the table where she was piling some plates on top of other plates. She was immersed in her chores.

"Adeline." He called from behind her. She stood up straight and for a moment she didn't turn around. "Can I talk to you?" He pleaded as she turned around and stared at him, almost frightened. He saw her eyes fill with tears. She was embarrassed. He could feel her pain, pain that he had caused her.

"Lanny." She said in a soft voice, he loved the way she said his name. "How...how..." But she was too choked with emotion to finish. Lanny gently took her by the elbow and led her over to the clean table and pulled out a chair for her to sit down. He observed her closely, her heart was pounding in her chest and her pulse was racing.

"Adeline, I came to say sorry." Lanny said in a low tone, aware that there was another nun in the back and two men were playing cards a short distance from them. The nun in the rear, looked out from the side of the tall refrigerator and carefully kept an eye on them.

"You have nothing to be sorry for." She whispered as she tried very hard not to cry in front of him. "I made a complete fool of myself." A rogue tear rolled down her face. Lanny wanted to take her in his arms and hold her close and never let her go.

"No, you didn't, it was I who behaved deplorably." Lanny admitted and felt even lower than he had since that night in his apartment. He reached for her hand and held it; he didn't care who saw them. It was soft and her skin was milk white. Lanny could see the blue vein bulge and then he looked into her green eyes. "I have to go away for a while but before I leave, I needed to apologise to you." She gazed lovingly at him and their eyes locked. It was a glance that he always loved whenever he had been alone with her.

"Why are you leaving?" She asked fretfully, and Lanny could hear the panic set in, in her voice.

"To recover from an illness, I picked up." He told her in a low tone and caressed her hand with his thumb. She was so stunning, so vulnerable.

"Was it from me?" She breathed. Lanny regarded her carefully. "The illness that you caught?"

"Yes," he grinned. "I felt a deep desire for you, that I shouldn't have and now I have to mend my broken heart." They both giggled, but he was being serious, and he didn't want to admit it. He had fallen in love with her, he couldn't deny that, not to her or to himself.

The council of Elders would discipline him severely for this, if they found out, Lanny felt sure that Demis, wouldn't wait to tell them. *Miserable old toad!*

"Will you be back, Lanny?" He picked up on the desperation in her voice. He felt desperate too, a despair he couldn't control. He glanced at her lovely face, her purity evident, a pureness that would always remind him of the monster that he had buried deep inside of him.

"Yes, and when I do return, if there is anything you need, just let me know." He stood up and she walked with him to the door. "Anything at all, Adeline." Lanny wanted to hold her close to him and never let her go. He knew that without her, he was empty, a shell but if he held her, she would see his behemoth appearance, and she would hate him for the monstrous creature that he was.

Lanny looked at her for a moment, she was such a beautiful, kind young woman and she would never know how much she meant to him.

He bent his head tempus kissed her softly on the forehead and smiled. "Goodbye, Adeline." And with that, Lanny opened the door and left.

As he was walking along the pavement, he heard his name called, he turned around and saw Demis. He looked despondent in his ill-fitting trousers and crinkled shirt, his black tie loose and his hair dishevelled.

"Are you ready, Jarl?" Demis asked and looked distastefully around at tent city.

"Just need to drop my car off at the Praetorian's garage, philosopher." Lanny said and glanced over his shoulder to the soup kitchen. He saw that Adeline was standing at the table where he had left her, she was looking after him.

Reluctantly Lanny opened the car door, and they got in and drove to Peo's place.

Chapter 33

The Militibus were sitting in Luca's office as they waited for Demis. He had told Luca that he needed to see them urgently and that it was important for all of them to be there. They were restless.

Peo was sitting with one leg resting over the other one and he was tapping his fingers on his calf. He wore a bored expression. Demis was always late and never showed up anywhere on time. He enjoyed wasting their time. Peo was tired of it.

Bjorn was sitting on the arm of the leather sofa deep in thought. Luca smiled across at his friends. They always came through for whatever was thrown at them. This case was no exception. He was proud of them.

As he glanced across at Lanny, he wondered what he was thinking of, as the expression that he wore didn't give anything away. It had been a difficult case for him, firstly he didn't trust the priest but what had surprised Luca, and the others was how invested he became in solving the crime. Luca knew that Lanny had paid a deep personal price with this one. But he showed true grit as he always did with his dedication to any case he investigated.

He had to go back to the Sixth dimension early to feed because he had succumbed to the age-old killer, he fell in love with a pure mortal woman. It could have destroyed him if he hadn't been as strong or determined as he was.

When he returned after his brief sojourn, he seemed better, more like the old Jarl they knew but Luca was aware that Lanny would always struggle where the nun was concerned. She would always be a challenge for him, how he dealt with it would define his strength of character.

"Good old Demis, always late." Bjorn grumbled as he drummed his fingers on his muscular thigh.

"What does the old fool want this time?" Peo joined in too, in the grumbling. They were like a pair of old hens pecking at whatever they could find to moan about.

"Cut him some slack." Lanny said as he grinned at them. "He has to have some excuse to come hang out with us." The all laughed.

"That is the worst thing you ever said, Jarl." Demis grumbled as he came into the room and dusted off his cloak. "To believe, I would want to hang out with a bunch of vampires."

"Nice outfit, philosopher." Lanny jibed, as he always did. "Very...you."

"Hmmm always the snob, Jarl." The four Militibus laughed loudly as they watched Demis as he sat down. He looked even more perturbed than usual. More worried and more disillusioned.

"What did you want to see us about Demis." Luca asked quickly as he handed him a glass of whiskey.

He took the glass and drank a long sip of the expensive amber liquid. He let out a long low sigh and then as if remembering where he was, he looked at the Militibus.

"Congratulations on a job well done. I understand the clergyman has been exemplified in his parish and has plans to open up more accommodation in the hotel."

"Yes, he is a very dedicated mortal." Lanny agreed and Luca watched him to see if there was any reason to be concerned about the budding friendship between Lanny and the priest. But he didn't see anything to be anxious about. They seemed to genuinely enjoy each other's company.

"Good, now Militibus," Demis looked almost dismayed, and his tone was very grave as he looked at his four officers. He had their full attention. "I have some very disturbing news." Demis said as he took a sip of whiskey.

"What is it, Demis?" Luca asked as he watched the older man, his bony fingers clasping the glass for dear life. He was miserable, more so than they were all accustomed to.

"You know that I have been custodian with the keys to the Tenth?" They all nodded. Demis was the gatekeeper to all the dimensions, and he was the key holder to the Tenth dimension, the dimension where all the souls of the most dangerous kind were imprisoned.

"What of it?" Lanny asked cautiously as he looked at his old friend in an irritated manner.

"The key to the Tenth has been stolen, Militibus," Demis blurted out in his dower voice. "Someone has taken it and if they open the gate, then by the gods, help this dimension, for a fate worse than hell will be unleashed."

The Militibus stared at each other and then over at the philosopher, they knew that the situation had just turned ominous, this was trouble.

Demis had, once more messed up!

The End